Carl Weber's:

Five Families of New York

Part 3: The Bronx

Carl Weber's:
Five Families of New York
Part 3: The Bronx

C. N. Phillips

URBAN
BOOKS

www.urbanbooks.net

Urban Books, LLC
300 Farmingdale Road, N.Y.-Route 109
Farmingdale, NY 11735

Carl Weber's: Five Families of New York Part 3: The Bronx
Copyright © 2022 C. N. Phillips

ISBN 13: 978-1-64556-284-9
ISBN 10: 1-64556-284-0

First Trade Paperback Printing March 2022
Printed in the United States of America

10 9 8 7 6 5 4 3 2 1

This is a work of fiction. Any references or similarities to actual events, real people, living or dead, or to real locales are intended to give the novel a sense of reality. Any similarity in other names, characters, places, and incidents is entirely coincidental.

Distributed by Kensington Publishing Corp.
Submit Orders to:
Customer Service
400 Hahn Road
Westminster, MD 21157-4627
Phone: 1-800-733-3000
Fax: 1-800-659-2436

Carl Weber's:
Five Families of New York
Part 3: The Bronx

by

C. N. Phillips

Prologue

Two Months Ago

The night sky lit up with lightning, and thunder followed closely after. DeMarco Alverez's feet splattered snow and slush on the ground with each step as he made his way down a dark alley. Halfway down the alley, a door to an old, worn-down building was open. Standing outside, awaiting the arrival of that night's guest, was an Asian man wearing a suit and hat.

"Marco," the man said, acknowledging him, and he nodded his head in greeting.

"Shen," Marco said, giving a nod back. "Where is your uncle?"

"Waiting for you, but first I must ask, were you followed?" Shen asked, looking over Marco's shoulder in the direction he'd just come from.

"I'm positive Caesar's hounds are nowhere near this location. I was careful," Marco responded, speaking of kingpin Caesar King's most loyal runners.

Shen studied Marco for a few moments before finally stepping out of the way and granting Marco entrance to the underground business. Shen's uncle, Li Zhang, ran the Bronx and was the head of one of the Five Families in New York. Marco was the head of his family's operation in Queens. The two of them meeting alone without the other families' accompaniment was completely unorthodox, which was why it was so important that Marco wasn't followed.

Marco walked closely behind Shen as he led him downstairs and through many different doors. Marco's line of business was providing weapons to the streets. Not the ones the CIA and other government entities provided and could track. He gave the people ghost guns. So it wasn't hard to understand that, in his trade, he had seen many things. But when he walked through one of the doors with Shen, he was shocked to see a man being tortured with many deadly instruments. He wasn't surprised he was being tortured. He was surprised to see who the man was.

Eric Summers had been one of Marco's buyers for years. Eric was a white man with sandy blond hair and a face the ladies went crazy over, or at least it had been. He was Caesar's executive distro, someone who could get product in places no one else could, like to the mayor and other government officials. His job was dangerous, which was why Marco had always provided him and his team with weapons. Marco didn't understand why he was tied up and bloody.

"Marco," Eric cried weakly. "Help me please. They're . . . they're going to kill me."

Marco paused briefly as he saw one of the Chinese men grab a long, skinny knife. Another went behind Eric and pulled his trousers down. Eric cried for Marco's help again, but he turned his head away. Shen motioned to a door on the other side of the room, and Marco walked through it, leaving Eric behind. Marco pretended he hadn't seen anything and kept his face blank and as uninterested as possible.

Next Shen took him through a room filled with naked Asian women giggling and snorting cocaine from each other's breasts. He didn't bat an eye. It wasn't until

Shen opened the door to a room where five Asian men were sitting at a table seemingly lost in conversation that Marco showed interest, mainly because the man he'd come to see was sitting there at the table. Upon his entrance, the other four men stood quickly and made a swift exit, leaving Marco, Li, Shen, and the security.

"Uncle, Marco has arrived, and I have brought him to you," Shen spoke respectfully. "Do you have any other use for me at this time?"

"No, dear nephew. Go find your brother Tao and assume your duties," Li told him.

Shen bowed at both Li and Marco in farewell before he left, closing the door behind him. Li, like Marco, was a man in his early sixties with a graying top coat of hair. His eyes never seemed to be fully open, but he was always paying attention. Marco sat at the round table across from Li and allowed his eyes to brush over the statue of Buddha in one of the corners of the room. Smoke from the lit incense swirled around him where he sat awaiting to know the reason Li had summoned him in secret.

"I am glad you came, Marco," Li started. "But I must say I am surprised to see you alone."

"My men stayed back. But I shouldn't need an entourage in your place of business, should I, Li? The Pact should keep me protected," Marco said with a childish smirk.

"Of course you are protected here," Li scoffed. "I would never threaten your safety. I was merely making an observation."

The Pact was an order stating that no member of the Five Families could do any harm to any member of the families or their affiliates. The act would be punishable by the harshest form of death. To Marco, it always seemed like a double standard, but it was one that made sense. The Five Families were to be allies, not enemies.

The Pact was put in place by Caesar to keep business going and money flowing. Each syndicate had its own niche, which meant that nobody stepped on each other's toes, and they all could do business with each other and in each other's boroughs.

At first, Li's father didn't agree to come together with the other families. In fact, he attempted one last fight with Caesar and lost. In the end, he agreed to serve under the Pact.

"To what do I owe this meeting? I have to say, Li, you've made me feel like what these kids today call a sneaky link."

"I wanted to meet with you in private and away from the others to discuss some matters at hand. One in particular."

"Then I can only assume you called me here to talk about the king himself, and that wasn't a play on his last name," Marco said. He adjusted his diamond cuff links before clasping his hands together on the table. "And if that's what we're here to discuss, my first question is going to be, why?"

"Caesar's self-appointment as the king of all of New York is alarming."

"When did he name himself the king of all of New York, or did I miss something? Because the last time I checked, I'm the king of Queens, and you're the king of the BX."

"Do not patronize me, Marco. You know exactly what I am talking about. Nothing is done without Caesar's approval. Manhattan is becoming more and more lucrative. We make him richer and richer every day. Maybe I'm wrong in thinking you feel how I feel."

"And how do we feel? Just so I can let you know if we're on the same page, amigo."

"Untrusting. He thinks that, just because he has more tenure running his borough, he has more authority than the rest of us. I fear his arrogance and immoral outlook on life will eventually lead us all astray and down a dark path."

"What makes you think he'll do something so reckless?"

"Greed. It's no secret that he wants to expand his reach from just Manhattan. Barry outed him for that years ago. And now that white devil shorts me on my monthly shipment from Caesar. It is the second time in a row it has happened."

"Eric?"

"Yes, Eric."

"I'm sure that was a misunderstanding. Did you tell Caesar?"

"Why would I need to tell Caesar about something coming directly from his camp? It was done purposely. I am tired of the scraps, and I am tired of being capped at only one trade. When my family came to New York, we did it all."

"All of our families did it all, but when the Pact was put into place, we agreed to a lane and that we would stay in it."

"It is a small bubble we are forced to stay in while Caesar plans to expand."

"I think expansion should be in everybody's sights. I sell weapons all over the world, I don't see anybody complaining." Marco shrugged. "And I'm positive that you do business in more than just New York, amigo."

"Of course I do! That is not the point I am trying to make. We should not have to depend on out-of-state money when New York is a gold mine. It's just split in five pieces. Pennies, that's what it is. It was a joke to think that an agreement like the one Caesar put in place would last."

"Enlighten me."

"The Pact *will* fall. Peace cannot last forever. There is a cosmic balance, and good never prevails. Especially when not all parties are happy."

"You aren't happy, Li?" Marco asked, and they stared at each other for a few seconds before Li gave a small smile.

"Let's just say I'm waiting for the day when it falls. And when it does, I don't plan on just sitting around while Caesar takes every territory in New York for himself. He's already shown that he wants more than one, and if he gets two, what's to stop him from getting three? And after that, who is to say he won't come for our houses next? His constant talk of expansion is worrisome for many reasons! And if you can't see this, then you are a fool. While we are abiding by his rules, who's to say he isn't planning an uprising?"

"Let's hypothetically say that the Pact does fall. Am I to believe that you would be content only with what you currently have? Or would you too attempt to control more than one borough like what you are saying Caesar would do?" Marco asked his question with an even tone.

"Queens would be safe," Li told him. "I'm not sure if I can speak for any other."

Marco sat and basked in the silence that soon followed Li's words. He could tell by the intense stare he was receiving that Li was truly alarmed. Whereas Marco didn't know if Caesar would ever abolish the Pact, there was some truth behind Li's fears. It wasn't any secret that Caesar had more power than the rest of them. Where he went, people followed.

"Only a fool would go against Caesar, Barry, and Diana," Marco finally said. "Their families will always stick together."

"And they would be fools to go against us," Li stated. "I did not bring you here to discuss starting a war . . . yet. I brought you here to make a proposition."

"What do you propose?"

"An alliance," Li said promptly. "We will have each other's word that we will come to each other's aid in business and in war. You will put my Family's needs first when it comes to providing us with any weapon we require. And you will be compensated greatly for it."

"What about the others?"

"What about them?" Li asked, taking a sip of his hot tea. "I have no trust in their self-interest at the moment. You said it yourself—they will always stick together. If they were in your position right now, the moment this meeting was over, they'd go running to tell Caesar about it. But you? You want to preserve your throne and your riches the same way I want to preserve mine."

"So basically you don't trust me, you trust my greed?"

"Simply put, yes."

"And what if the Pact stays in place?"

"Then you might not have anything to worry about. I see nothing wrong with, how do you Americans put it, having all bases covered. You'll have my eyes, and I'll have yours. You'll have my army, and I'll have yours. What do you say? Do I have your word, Marco?"

Li extended his hand, and Marco looked at it. His jaw clenched mainly because Li was basically asking Marco to go against Caesar. That was a dangerous game to play. The Kings were the only family to go up against every other family and win every time. But Marco also knew what was in his own personal interest.

"You have my word." Marco took Li's hand in his and gave it a firm shake before letting it go. He stood up and began making his exit. "Now I should get back to my men outside. I told them I'd be out in twenty minutes, and if I don't show, well, you know the rest. But first, I have one last question."

"Ask."

"Earlier, you said the Pact *will* fall. Is there anything I should know about?" Marco's brow crinkled slightly, and Li smirked.

"We will be in touch," was all he said, and he nodded his farewell.

Without another word, Marco left the room. Instead of Shen, two of Li's other nephews escorted him out the same way he'd come in. That time when he passed through the room with the naked women, one of them grabbed his arm.

"You look like you could use a good time," she said in a soft voice and showed off her petite frame.

Marco's eyes fluttered to her perky breasts and their pink nipples. Behind her, the other girls were pleasuring themselves on the tables and couches for him to see. Marco was a man who enjoyed the company of women, so of course he felt himself get an erection. But he was also a man who was disciplined, and he couldn't care less about getting his dick wet when there were more important matters at hand.

"If you choose to partake, our uncle would like you to know it is on the house," one of Li's nephews said to him.

"Generous offer, really. But I need to get going," Marco said and continued on his way, leaving the women with disappointed pouts on their faces.

When he was outside of the building, he walked back down the alley where a car was awaiting his return. The rain had stopped, but he could still smell it in the muggy air. Behind him, he could feel Li's nephews' eyes on him, but when he neared the end of the alley, he heard the door shut. He glanced over his shoulder and saw that they, in fact, were gone. He let out a breath that seemed to have been just sitting in his chest.

Li had been right to assume that Marco would always side with the best decision for his family. He had been right to bet on Marco's greed. He had made one mistake though. And that was not questioning what Marco thought was in his best interests. The back door of the awaiting vehicle opened, and Marco slid inside. His door wasn't shut but a brief moment when the car started driving away from the Chinese territory. He was not alone in the back seat. On the other side was a man shielded by the shadows of the passing buildings.

"You were right," Marco said to him. "Li can't be trusted."

"Usually I hate when a man tells me something that I already know."

Caesar King leaned out of the shadows just enough so that Marco could see his face. He didn't look angry, but he didn't seem happy either. The expression on his face was neutral.

"There's something else. You're going to need a new distro. They have Eric, and I doubt he'll be alive by the morning. Li said he was shorting his supply."

Caesar briefly closed his eyes and exhaled.

"That's my fault. Governor Wilkins said that we were shortchanging him, too, but I thought the fat motherfucker was being greedy. Eric must have been skimming off the top and selling on the side. I should have looked into it, but I didn't. Let me guess—Li thinks I ordered Eric to do that."

"It's looking that way," Marco said and looked Caesar in the eyes. "There was a reason you wanted me to accept Li's invitation tonight. You might have known that he wasn't somebody you can trust, but you also needed proof for that theory."

"You're right, and I'm guessing now you have that proof. What did he want?"

"To tell me that he doesn't trust you either," Marco told him. "He doesn't trust that the Pact will hold up, and he's convinced that you are out trying to expand."

"Of course I'm trying to expand. A lion doesn't become king by staying under a tree," Caesar said with a chuckle.

"In New York," Marco finished, and the smile left Caesar's lips. "Li thinks you're out for more than the one borough you agreed to control in New York."

"And what do you think?" Caesar asked with his eyes on Marco's.

"I can tell you what I don't think. I don't think the man who ended the war among all five houses would have done so just to start it again," Marco said, and Caesar sighed in relief.

"And you would be right," Caesar said. "But I would be wrong to lie and tell you that Staten Island hasn't always been in my sights. However, we would all benefit from that acquisition. My mind is always on growing, but I also know that we are stronger together. Any decision I make will always be for all of our best interest. And that's why we vote on these things. Li going behind my back lets me know that he may have something else stirring in the pot, which is why I hope you accepted his offer."

"I did."

"Good. I'll feed you information to report to him, and you'll tell me anything you hear going on in his camp. In return, you will be compensated—"

"I don't want you to pay me for doing what's in the best interest of the families," Marco cut him off. "I'm not going to keep my eyes on him just for you. I'm doing it for all of the families. Something isn't right."

"The way I see it is we'll either find out one day, or we won't. Either way, I won't let the families fall."

Chapter 1

Boogie Tolliver didn't know if it was the Chinese men shooting their guns at the house he was in, or the fact that he didn't have any of his own shooters at his disposal, that had his heart racing. He looked to his god-father and New York kingpin, Caesar King, knowing he wouldn't be much help in a fight. He was still too weak. Same with Diana, Caesar's colleague and Harlem's queen. As she stood near him looking out the window too, he saw her clenching the bandages over the bullet wound she'd sustained in a recent battle. He wouldn't let her get hurt anymore, especially when he was the one they wanted.

Boogie was the one who'd killed the leader of the Chinese syndicate. Li had been seated as the head of his Family and had controlled the Bronx for years before Boogie put an end to it. Boogie had been blinded by rage and revenge, and now everyone was paying for his mistakes. Caesar, Diana, and Marco might have forgiven him, but he knew the Chinese never would.

"Did y'all hear that? What's going on?" Morgan, Diana's daughter and Boogie's sister, said, rushing into the room.

"It looks like the Chinese have come back to repay a debt," Diana said. "They're here to avenge their fallen."

"And I'm about to give them what they want," Boogie said and started toward the bedroom door.

"No, the hell you aren't," Caesar stepped in and grabbed his arm, preventing him from taking another step. "Are you out of your mind, boy?"

"It's my fault Li's dead! If they get me, you'll all live."

"Boy, shut your damn mouth before I rethink letting a dumbass run Harlem while I rest," Diana chimed in. "You aren't going out there with those savages!"

"But they're angry because I killed Li!"

"Ask yourself something, Boogie." Diana stared into his face. "This is supposed to be a secret location. You only found out about it today. So tell me how all of those Chinese men out there knew where to find us if Li is dead?"

Boogie sat on the question for a moment before the answer came to him. "Because they already knew."

"Right. They already knew where it was. And I'm thinking that Li told them about the Big House when I was first brought here after your mother shot me," Caesar said to Boogie. "And the only reason he would have done that is because—"

"He was targetin' you," Boogie said and shook his head. "But why?"

"Why does anyone target the strongest of the pack?" Caesar asked.

"Am I missing something?" Diana asked.

"Let's just say sometimes our enemies are closer than we think."

"Great story time, but we need to be focusing on what we're going to do right now," Morgan butted in. "We can discuss all of that later. In the meantime, how the hell are we going to get out of here?"

"Through the front door," Caesar said calmly and let Boogie's arm go.

He left the room with Marco assisting Diana right behind him. Boogie and Morgan looked at each other before rushing after them to the main level of the house. There they were met by Boogie's right-hand man, Bentley, and Bentley's cousin, Gino, who joined them in following

Caesar. Their guns were drawn, and they had concerned looks on their faces.

"Ay, you see that shit outside?" Bentley asked.

"Yeah."

"They're after you?"

"Yup."

"Because you had their mans toasted." Gino blurted out the obvious, and Morgan glared at him. "What? You know it's true just like I know it's true. My nigga had that man ripped to shreds. But fuck it, Boog. You know I'm riding until the wheels fall off."

"No wheels will be falling off today," Caesar called over his shoulder when he finally reached his destination in the Big House.

They were standing outside of a big red door with a lock on it. Caesar unlocked it with a chain of keys he pulled from his pocket and pushed the door open, revealing the house's control room. On the walls were many TV monitors that had surveillance of the whole house, inside and outside. Caesar took a seat behind a computer, which seemed to be the main control center, and picked up a mic. They all filed inside behind him, and Marco helped Diana take a seat on a couch against the wall. Boogie stood near Caesar, curious to see what he was about to do.

"This is Caesar King," Caesar said, speaking into the mic. Upon the sound of his voice, on one of the monitors the Chinese men were seen looking around. "By the look of surprise on your faces, you can hear me, and if you come to the door and talk into the mic, I'll be able to hear you too. What can I do for you on this fine day?"

The Chinese men looked at each other before one of them stepped forward and went to the door. He walked cautiously and didn't look to be much older than Boogie.

"That's Tao's son, Ming," Marco whispered to Caesar.

"I recognize him," Caesar said, speaking away from the mic. "The last time I saw him, he was a boy."

"He ain't no boy anymore. Tao turned him into a cold-blooded killer. He's one of their most skilled hands," Marco said right before Ming started speaking.

"I am Ming Zhang, great-nephew of Li Zhang. You want to know what I want?" His voice filled the room through the speakers on the ceiling. He was soft-spoken, but his tone carried a certain chill with it. It was the kind that made the hairs on the back of your neck stand up. "I want you to count the seconds before I kill you. And then I'm going to kill everyone you love since I am told that you have sided with the Tolliver boy, who is responsible for my great-uncle's death."

"Yes. I have sided with my godson," Caesar confirmed. "I've decided to back him up in whatever is to come."

"Then you'll die beside him as well," Ming sneered. "Your sacred Pact is broken! You have no honor."

"That could be debated," Caesar told him. "But in the meantime, I'm going to kindly ask for you to leave this property."

"Not until there is blood on my hands!" Ming shouted and hit the door with his fist.

"Then it might come as a disappointment to know that this entire house is reinforced. It would take many tanks to penetrate the walls. But if you insist on having blood, I can give you your own."

Caesar's voice was calm as he pressed a command button on the computer. Boogie watched as big guns expelled from high on the brick exterior of the house. There were four of them, and they were aimed directly at Ming and his men.

"What is this?" Ming demanded.

"A warning. All I have to do is press one more button and those guns will make your bodies rock harder than they ever have before. Take your men home, and live to fight another day," Caesar told him.

Ming looked at the guns and stepped away from the door. The one pointed at him followed his every move, keeping a red dot on his chest. He let out a frustrated shout before turning his back and violently gesturing to his men to get back into their cars. One by one they left until finally the coast was clear.

"What a shame. I was finally looking forward to using that security measure. Maybe next time," Caesar said, getting up. "In the meantime, Marco, call us an escort. We need to leave here immediately. Bentley, please round up the nurses and *persuade* them into not speaking about what happened today."

"Okay," Marco said, pulling out his phone.

"Got it." Bentley left the room.

"The rest of you, go home," Caesar instructed. "The safest place for you right now is with your own house. My plan had been to stay dead to the world, but I think it's time to resume my position."

Boogie and all the rest nodded their heads. Well, all but Diana. She stared at Caesar with the eyes of a hawk, and when they began to file out of the control room, she stayed. And because she stayed, Boogie did too.

"Go help get Tazz ready for transport," he told Morgan. "I'll be there in a second."

When it was just the three of them, Boogie watched Caesar and Diana curiously. There was something going on between them at the moment that he couldn't quite put his finger on. Caesar sighed even before Diana opened her mouth.

"Ask what you need to ask."

"Is there anything you need to tell me?" She eyed him curiously.

"When the time is right, I'll tell you. But right now we need to focus on putting up a good defense."

"This is all my fault," Boogie groaned and clenched his fists. "If I hadn't been so quick to fight instead of figure the shit out, we wouldn't be here. When I think back on all that happened with my pops, it was all there. Right in front of my face."

"Don't blame yourself for being blinded by people you trusted and loved. This is Julius and Dina's fault. They started a war and used you as the face of it. They broke the Pact, not you," Diana said, speaking of Boogie's mother and his father's right-hand man, who was also dead. She turned to Caesar. "You made some pretty heavy accusations not too long ago. You think Li wanted you dead?"

"Why else would people in his camp know about this location? And as you just heard, he thought I was here alone."

"But why would Li want to kill you?

"For the same thing you wanted—to be in control of all five territories."

"That's ridiculous." Diana shook her head in disbelief. "Li never showed interest in anything of the sort."

"Sometimes the eyes have to pay attention to what's not shown outwardly but what's being done in the background."

"If you felt like this, why didn't you say anything before?" Diana asked, clutching her side.

"I never got the opportunity to prove it. I was so busy trying to find out who killed Barry that I forgot about the potential other dog at my stoop. And then there's the matter of me, you know, almost dying."

"You're saying a lot without saying anything, Caesar." Diana eyed him suspiciously. "There's something you aren't telling me."

"All I want for you to do is get better. We're old, Diana. Focus on regaining your strength."

"So now what?" Boogie asked. "We prepare for another war?"

"Yes." Caesar nodded. "Tao will be named the new head of his family, and he will be out for retribution. There are things about the Chinese family that nobody knows. We need to prepare for the worst."

Chapter 2

Knock! Knock!

"Come in," Tao Chen said with very little effort.

He was busy soaking in the spa area of his lavish home. Joined with him in the hot tub were two beautiful naked Asian women. They were pleasuring each other in front of him, and that in turn pleasured him. He wasn't annoyed at the disturbance. After all, he was expecting his son to return with news that would make him smile from ear to ear. He grabbed a towel and wrapped it around his waist before getting out of the hot tub.

"Hello, Father," Ming said when he entered.

He sat down at one of the tables on the side of the spa and avoided his father's eyes. The look on his face wasn't one of a man who successfully completed a mission. It was a look of defeat. Tao took a seat across from his son at the small circular table. He watched him with his dark brown eyes while the women moaned and giggled in the background. Ming was the spitting image of his mother, which Tao had always hated. His mother was a beautiful woman, but her features made Ming look too soft. He had always been too handsome for his own good, which was why Tao made the decision early to turn him into a hardened killer. His looks had been made into a weapon. Anyone would trust his face, especially his eyes. That is, until those same eyes were watching as his victim took their last breath.

"I demand that my son look at me," he said briskly, and Ming slowly turned his gaze to his father. Tao studied the perfectly pressed white collared shirt under Ming's blazer. "I expected you to enter this spa with blood on your shirt. But instead you sit across from me looking like you are late for a photo shoot."

"I let you down today, Father."

"What happened?" Tao asked.

"We weren't able to kill Caesar King. And he has made it known that he sides with the Tolliver family."

"He said this to your face?"

"Not exactly. He spoke from a speaker. We did not get inside of the house," Ming said, and Tao gave a small smile.

In a perfect world, Tao would have been a loving and supportive father. He would have been there with arms wide open whenever his son got a cut or a bruise. He would have offered him advice when he got his heart broken by a girl for the first time, and encouraged him to go off to college to get his doctorate. But that kind of father was something he could never be. He was raising a soldier, a hardened man fit to take over an entire empire when it was his time. Quickly Tao wound his hand back and slapped Ming across the face so hard that he left a red handprint.

"You are worthless to me," Tao said. "You could not even handle a simple task."

"It was not simple, Father! You told us where the house was, not that it was enforced or had those kinds of upgrades. Our bullets did no damage to the house at all! We would have all died just trying to get inside!"

"I would rather have your corpse in front of me than a failure!"

"You . . . you don't mean that," Ming said, but it almost sounded like a question.

Tao sighed. The truth was that he didn't know anything about the Big House, just where it was. And his uncle had only just told him the location of it as well as of Caesar's survival right before he died. He had sent his son in blind, and if he *had* died, Ming's blood would have been on his hands. He wasn't a sentimental father, but he was a thorough general. And even he had to admit that would have been a senseless death.

"Maybe I don't, but next time I want results."

"Yes, Father." Ming nodded quickly.

"We are at war, Ming. And that means every small battle counts. It's funny, Uncle always feared Caesar becoming the controlling head of two of New York's major territories. He never gave it a thought that the Tolliver family would be the one to actually do it. Not before he himself did anyway. Uncle was a selfish man, but he was also cunning. He grew tired of living someone else's idea of harmony long ago. Do you know why?"

"Why?"

"Because someone else's harmony will always have a cap. And freedom should not have a limit. It should be limitless. Boogie's war gave us the key and unlocked the door to our freedom. Uncle paid for it with his life, and Boogie will pay for that by bowing down to the new king of New York. Me. Out with the old ways, and in with the new—my new. Now please go do something right and have our staff get the guest living quarters ready. Our guest will be here soon."

Chapter 3

"Ooh, Nicky. I forgot how big you were," a butter-pecan goddess said while grinding on Nicky King's manhood.

Cheshire had always been one of Nicky's favorite pastimes, but he hadn't had time to see her in a while. She had a voluptuous body and a wide, perfect smile, just like the Cheshire Cat's, which was where she'd gotten her stage name at the Sugar Trap. He'd called her up to help take the edge of failure off.

Nicky was still writhing from the fact that Boogie had gotten the best of him in the way he had the last time the two men were face-to-face. He'd made Nicky look weak and like a fool. Not only that, but many of Nicky's shooters were killed in the process. Having to tell their mothers, wives, and babies' mothers that they weren't coming home was the sorriest thing he'd had to do in a long time. He vowed that he would get Boogie back.

"Ahh! Yessss!" Cheshire moaned when Nicky began thrusting upward and deep inside of her.

Their skin slapped against each other's, and one of his hands gripped her thick bottom while the other fondled her breast. With each stroke he felt himself growing nearer to his climax. He felt her walls contract on his shaft and the shiver of her body. An ocean of her juices flowed down on his torso, and he couldn't hold it in any longer. His hand went from her breast to her neck, and he squeezed as a growl escaped his lips. He came powerfully into his condom and felt his eyes roll to the back of his head. Cheshire always gave him the best sex, and that time was no exception.

"Whew, I missed that dick!" Cheshire fell next to him on the king-sized bed. "Nicky, you fuck me so good, baby."

Nicky caught his breath for a few minutes and then opened his eyes. He wanted to tell her to go and grab him a towel and a drink from his fridge, but as he looked around, he remembered one thing. They weren't even at his house. He'd been staying at his uncle Caesar's mansion a few nights a week ever since he died. He had his own room in the grand home, but that afternoon he had taken Cheshire on a spin in the master bedroom, aka Caesar's room. He hadn't meant to sex Cheshire on the bed like that. He'd only wanted to show her his uncle's gun collection. Apparently guns turned Cheshire on, because the next thing Nicky knew, she was on all fours gobbling his dick up in that wet mouth of hers. And the rest was history.

"Get up and get dressed," Nicky said, getting up from the bed. He went into the master bathroom to flush the condom and wash his hands. When he came back, he saw that Cheshire was still naked in the same place he left her. "Yo, for real. Get up. If my cousin catches us in here, she'll kill us."

Milli, short for Amelia, was Caesar's only child. She had taken his death hard and hated for anybody to be by his bedroom door, let alone inside his room. She would blow a head gasket if she knew what Nicky had just done, which was why she couldn't find out.

Nicky picked up Cheshire's clothes and threw them on the bed next to her. She snatched them up with a bit of an attitude, but Nicky was too busy pulling his clothes back on to notice. He was buttoning his shirt up, and she finally sashayed past him, fully dressed. Nicky was given another look of how edible her butt looked in her dress and was reminded of how they'd gotten there in the first place. Nicky remade the bed and made sure there were no wrinkles in the cover before throwing his blazer over his shoulder and leaving the room with Cheshire.

"Take the elevator," he told her and handed her a wad of $100 bills. "For your troubles. If you run into anyone on your way out, just say you were here with me."

"Okay." She took the money and kissed him on the cheek.

He waited until she was inside of the golden elevator at the end of the grand hallway and for the doors to shut to head for the stairwell in the opposite direction. He bounded down the stairs feeling the guilt in his chest get a little heavier. He hadn't meant to disrespect his uncle's memory, not just by having sex in his room, but by not killing Boogie. He had failed Caesar. How could he be expected to be a good leader when the first mission as such was a failure?

Nicky looked at the gold AP on his wrist and saw that it was two thirty in the afternoon. A meeting was supposed to be taking place in the basement of the mansion in an hour to discuss the next course of action, but Nicky needed to get some air before then. Cheshire had helped to clear his lower head, but the one on his shoulders could use some guidance. And the only person he trusted to give him that was long gone.

Nicky threw his blazer on when he reached the foyer and reached for his coat.

"I saw that ho sneaking out of here," his cousin Milli's voice said, creeping up behind him.

"Did you say anything to her?" Nicky asked, turning to face her.

"I told her to fix her walk and posture before she walked up out of here. If she's gonna fuck in a mansion, she should at least have some class about herself."

"I'm guessing she didn't take that too well," Nicky said with a sheepish grin.

"Nope. I'm sure you'll be getting a call from her soon," Milli said with a shrug. "Why is it always hoes you decide to deal with? Why don't you find a nice girl to settle down with?"

"Because those kinds of women require too much of my time. Which is to be expected. If I meet a good woman, I would want to treat her in a way that I just can't right now. A ho, on the other hand, takes what you give her, and it's done. That's all I have time for right now. Especially with having to take over for your old man."

"Well, all I'm saying is that this mansion could use some babies running around it."

"Then give it some," Nicky joked.

"One day," Milli said dreamily. "But right now I have to focus on my studies."

"That's right! Unc's ghost ain't gon' haunt me if you get knocked up."

"Oh, shut up!" Milli said with a laugh. "Where are you going anyways? Don't you boys have a meeting in a little bit? Nathan is already down there."

"Of course he is. My little brother is always punctual when it comes to business. But me? I need some air real quick. I'll be back on time."

"Mm-hmm. I'm getting Italian catered. I'll put your plate to the side. Make sure you're back on time, though."

"I will be. What's that your dad always said?" Nicky said, opening the front door and looking back at Milli. He didn't even notice that there was somebody standing on the other side. "If—"

"'If you're on time, then you're late.'"

The deep voice made Nicky freeze. His entire being recognized it, but it couldn't be. Slowly he turned around and inhaled in disbelief when he saw Caesar standing in front of him, very much alive.

"Unc?"

"Are you going to stare at me shit-faced, or are you going to give me a hug, boy?" Caesar asked, and he didn't have to do so twice.

Nicky had a swarm of emotions as he embraced Caesar, but mainly he felt a happiness so heavy that he couldn't put it into words. The two men patted each other's backs hard before pulling away.

"Daddy?" Milli inched forward. She too was in utter shock. The tears were streaming from her eyes, and her bottom lip quivered. "Is that really you?"

"Yes, baby girl, it's me."

"But how? They found your body."

"That wasn't me, baby girl. I've been here. And oh, how I've missed you," Caesar said and held his arms out to her.

She was like a little girl as she ran into his arms. She squeezed him tightly and sobbed into his neck. He held her in that doorway for as long as she needed him to. When she finally let him go, her eyes were bloodshot, and her bottom lip still shook. But anyone could tell how much joy she felt seeing her father.

"Come in!" she said, grabbing his arm and pulling him inside his home by the fur on his coat. Once they were inside of the foyer, Milli hugged her father again. "Are you hungry? You look skinny, Daddy."

"I could eat."

"Okay, let me go make you something real quick before the caterers get here."

"Caterers?"

"Nicky and the boys are having a meeting in a little bit. I ordered Italian, but I won't make you wait."

"Don't you want to hear about where I've been?" Caesar asked, and she shook her head.

"I don't care. All I know is that God brought you back to me, and that's all that matters. I'll be right back. Please still be here."

"I'm not going anywhere ever again, baby," he assured her, and she nodded with a teary smile.

When Nicky and Caesar were left alone, a silence fell over them. Nicky took that moment to really take his uncle in. Although the black fur coat Caesar wore over his suit was big, he could tell that Milli was right. He had lost a lot of weight. Not alarmingly, but his face definitely had more definition. Nothing had changed about his eyes though. In fact, they looked more determined right then than Nicky had ever seen them. Caesar reached over and patted Nicky lovingly on the cheek a few times.

"How have you been getting along without me, my boy?" he asked.

"It's been hard," Nicky admitted, suddenly feeling a lump form in the back of his throat. "But it's good to see you. I thought . . . we thought . . ."

"I know," Caesar sighed. "I know."

"Then how? Don't get me wrong, I'm almost in tears seeing you alive in front of me. But how is it possible? And why are you just now showing your face?"

"There's a lot to tell and a lot to take in, nephew. And honestly, I only want to tell the story once," Caesar said and gave Nicky a look that said "later."

"Okay. Everybody should be arriving up soon. Then you can tell us all together."

"Sounds like a plan. Where were you headed off to before I showed up?"

"I was . . . I was just goin' to go clear my head. A lot has happened since you died. I mean, I guess you didn't really die, but when I thought you were gone, everything fell on my shoulders. I wasn't ready."

"And that's my fault. I'll take accountability for that. I should have groomed you more. I was—"

"Busy running around with Boogie, grooming him," Nicky said and instantly felt guilty for his envy.

He'd just gotten his uncle back, but he would be a liar if he pretended he didn't feel a way about it. At first Caesar looked taken aback not just at the words, but the forcefulness of them. But quickly that wore off.

"I deserve that. There's a lot you don't know, and that once again is my fault."

"Like what?"

"You'll find out in a little bit, but first I'm going to go spend some time with my daughter. When everybody gets here, make sure they put their guns on the big table. Especially Nathan."

Chapter 4

The silence that fell across the basement was deafening. There were ten men, and each was overly cautious about making a sound, let alone moving. They were all too busy staring at Caesar. He was too busy eyeing his basement and making sure his *Scarface* posters were still intact on the walls to care too much. They were, and everything else was just like he'd left it. And as he'd requested, on a table along the far left wall were every guest's guns.

Caesar finished surveying the room and turned back to the men. He assumed his people didn't speak because they didn't know what to say. It wasn't every day that they saw somebody return from the dead. He sat in his normal seat facing his family, and he tried to fight the urge to laugh. It was just that their faces were so priceless he wished he could take a picture. Suddenly it hit him that maybe they were all waiting for him to speak.

"I'm sure you boys have a lot of questions, especially with all the noise in the streets of New York as of late," he said, breaking the silence.

"I only have one question—how?" His nephew Nathan spoke from where he was leaned against the bar. "I mean, they said they found your body on the news. If it wasn't you, why'd they say that?"

"Because they had no clue who they found." Caesar shrugged. "The body was burned. And when I didn't turn up, it was easy to say it was me. What's a better story than finding New York's kingpin dead in such a fashion?"

"We mourned you," Nathan said, and Caesar noticed the disdain in his voice. "I mean, if you were alive this whole time, where you been at? You abandoned us."

Of Nathan and Nicky, Nathan was the hotheaded brother. He had never learned to control his emotions, which made him the perfect soldier. However, when it came to placing his sadness, he never could. It always turned to anger. Caesar knew that both Nathan and Nicky loved him like a father, but whereas Nicky was just happy to see Caesar again, Nathan was angered by his absence. Caesar knew he would be, which was why he let Nathan's comment slide.

"It wasn't safe for me to reveal my survival to the world," Caesar said, speaking to him and the entire room of men. "I might not have died, but someone indeed tried to kill me. I'll spare you all the boring details, but just know it was better this way. And now that I'm back, I'm back. And there are more important things at hand that we need to discuss."

"Yeah, like how glad we are that you're back and seated on the throne. While you were gone, this nigga was left in charge," Jerrod, one of Caesar's little cousins, spoke up and shot Nicky a distasteful look. "He couldn't even handle one mission. He got Terrance and Blakey killed tryin'a get at Boogie."

"We all wanted to get at Boogie," Nathan said, jumping to his brother's defense.

"Yeah, well, the shot he called got my niggas killed." Jerrod puffed out his chest and stood.

That was the wrong thing to do to a roughneck like Nathan, who was always ready for a scuffle. He moved from the bar quickly and took a step toward Jerrod before Nicky jumped up from his seat beside Caesar to intervene. He knew that if Nathan got one punch off, it would be lethal.

"Chill out, bro," Nicky said, reaching him and putting a hand on his little brother's chest. "He ain't worth it. All he's good for is talking that shit."

"Well, in this case, I ain't talkin' shit. It's a fact. You got them killed because you went into a situation blind. Ol' stupid ass."

"In his defense, we all underestimated Boogie," Caesar calmly interjected. "Terrance and Blakey were like family even though they weren't blood. I'll be sure to send their mothers a check."

"That's it? That's all you have to say?" Jerrod asked incredulously. "Those were my friends! And this stupid motherfucka Nicky—"

"Jerrod, need I remind you that you married into this family, and I never liked your mother? Sit down, now!" Caesar cut him off icily, and Jerrod did what he was told with clenched jaws. "Nicky is my blood, and the most fit of any of you to lead. And now that I'm back, he'll be my right hand."

"Thanks, Unc," Nicky said and shook his head. "But what Jerrod says is the truth. I have my own people's blood on my hands."

"Jerrod is a dumb fuck who don't know when to shut up," Nathan spat out and glared at his cousin. "How was he supposed to know Boogie had that block sewn up with snipers on the rooftops?"

"Boogie had snipers on the rooftops?" Caesar asked, impressed.

"He did. For blocks, too. I barely made it out of there," Nicky said. "Unc, that nigga is a problem. And we need to deal with it. I heard he has Staten Island on lock now. Ain't no tellin' who he's over there getting in good with. We gotta take him out!"

"Yeah, Unc. And now that you're back, the streets are gon' know what's up. Boogie included!" Nathan said.

Caesar sighed when everybody in the room agreed with him. What he had to say, Nicky wasn't going to like. And if he wasn't going to like it, Nathan was going to hate it. Whenever the name Boogie was brought up, Caesar could see the contempt in their eyes for him. He couldn't blame them for it, either. Boogie had done some things that were unforgivable to most. He had let the evil inside of him run free, and although he had caged it, some might not be able to unsee him in that light. But that was neither here nor there. They all had an even bigger threat.

"Nephews, we need to talk."

"About what?" Nicky asked and then pointed at the big table with all of their guns. "And why did we have to disarm? You never like us to be naked."

"We need to talk about Boogie. He's—"

"Right here," a voice said from the direction of the stairs. Sure enough, Boogie was standing there with a small entourage of his people. "Sorry I'm late."

Chapter 5

"Ay yo, Unc! What the fuck is he doing here?" Nicky exclaimed, jabbing a finger at Boogie.

The entire room erupted into an uproar. Boogie's cousin Tazz and his right-hand man, Bentley, stepped in front of him just in case anyone tried to charge at him. Although Tazz was still injured, he refused to let Boogie go to the front line without him. He told Boogie that as long as his shooting hand still worked, he would defend him with his life. Nicky reached instinctively for his waist, but when he felt nothing but air, he cursed. He looked at the table that was completely covered with guns. Boogie felt the amusement inside of him, so he knew it showed on his face.

"Unc, please tell me this is some kind of joke. Why is he here?" Nicky asked again angrily.

"He's here because I invited him," Caesar said, standing and looking from Boogie back to Nicky. "Now you see why I wanted everyone to disarm."

"Sorry, Unc. Not everybody did," Nathan said, stepping forward.

He lifted his shirt and removed a Smith & Wesson 9 mm pistol that was strapped to his chest. Everyone, including Caesar, looked surprised. Right as Nathan aimed it for Boogie's head, Tazz had a beam in the center of his. Both men glared dangerously at each other and knew that the other wasn't bluffing with their guns. Nathan's reputation wasn't one Boogie took lightly. However, neither was Tazz's. Both men were lethal, and if they got to shooting, they were definitely going to hit their intended targets.

"By the time you shoot me, your man will already be dead," Nathan told him, and Nicky stood defiantly beside him.

"Chill out, little nigga, before I turn your face into linguine pasta," Tazz warned.

"We didn't come here for all that. We came here to talk business," Boogie said.

"What business? You spilled blood, nigga. If you ain't here to cash in for that, then you have no business."

"I did what I had to do when I thought what I was doing was right," Boogie said, and Nathan tried to comprehend his words.

"Nigga, what?" he asked and jabbed his gun. "I'm about to kill this fool, man."

"You won't be doing any such thing," Caesar told his nephew.

Boogie was glad he spoke up, but he hadn't moved an inch. Caesar had gone back to leaning in his chair and had even lit a Cuban cigar while they quarreled. Nathan looked like an angry child whose father had just told him he couldn't have a cookie. He still had his gun pointed at Boogie, but after Caesar spoke, he took his finger off the trigger.

"He broke the Pact!" he shouted.

"The Pact was broken when my father was killed," Boogie said through clenched teeth.

"And from what I hear, that was your own camp's doing," Nicky said, and upon hearing the words, Boogie's face softened.

"That's true," Boogie admitted. "But at the time, I didn't know that. I thought . . . I thought—"

"He thought I killed Barry, and with good reason," Caesar added, taking a puff of the cigar.

"By the time I realized that I was wrong, it was too late," Boogie said, looking Nicky square in the eye. "There are casualties in every war, and I can't bring those people back. But I can offer peace and help rebuild. That's one of the reasons why I'm here. The last time you and I were face-to-face like this, we were enemies. I come to you now as an ally."

Sincerity dripped from his voice, and to show good faith, he nodded for Tazz to lower his weapon. Tazz hesitated at first, but reluctantly he did what he was told. Nicky didn't seem the slightest bit moved, and Boogie thought he knew why. He'd embarrassed Nicky on the battlefield, and loss was a tough pill to swallow for any man with an ego. He was feeling like showing up to Caesar's was a mistake, but then Nicky surprised him. He still had a hard facial expression, but he placed a hand on top of Nathan's gun and forced his brother to lower it.

"Nathan, when Caesar says no guns, no guns. You disobeyed an order," he said and nodded toward the table.

Nathan wearily went to drop the gun on the table with the rest of them. He avoided eye contact with Caesar, who was staring at him like a hawk. Boogie hated to think about how that conversation would go later. The only thing that was important was the conversation right then and there.

"Are y'all serious? You aren't about to handle this nigga? He's right there!" a voice Boogie didn't recognize said.

The man speaking looked to be around Boogie's age. Although Boogie didn't recognize him, he recognized the look of hatred in his eyes. Like Boogie had taken something from him.

"We killed somebody you knew," Boogie stated. It wasn't a question.

"You did, and nothin' would make me happier than seein' your lungs outside of your chest," the man spat.

"I don't know your name," Boogie told him.

"Jerrod, nigga."

"You misunderstand me. I wasn't asking for it, so shut the fuck up talking to me before I bury you just like my snipers did yo' niggas," Boogie said and then turned back to Nicky. "The way I see it is we can all get back on the same page, or we can war forever. But one, I don't want to be at odds with my godfather anymore. And two, I'm the only motherfucka in this room who's runnin' three territories."

And just like that, Boogie set himself apart from the rest, including Nicky. And it was felt throughout the room like a whisk of brisk air. He wasn't one of them, and he felt the need to remind them. He wasn't a runner or a right-hand man. He was a boss. The boss. Diana's people seemed to understand that right off the bat, so it wasn't hard to gain their allegiance or take over for her while she healed. Plus it probably helped that he had spared them for his love of her. However, Caesar's people seemed a little harder to crack, which was understandable. But he had to remember he'd already shown them what he was capable of. He'd already beaten them. He wondered if that was how Caesar had felt when he was a teenager left in charge, after he beat all of the Families and realized all of the fighting just wasn't worth it.

"Godfather?" Nicky asked and looked from Caesar to Boogie.

"You heard right." Caesar nodded. "Boogie is my godson. And that makes him as much my family as you and Nathan. I have forgiven him because at one point I *was* him. We need to work together."

"Are you sure we can trust him? Didn't he kill Li? How do you know he won't do the same to you?"

"Because he's my family. And also if Boogie hadn't killed Li, I would have been forced to," Caesar said. Nicky looked surprised at Caesar's words and so did everyone else in the room besides Boogie. "If you boys are done trying to prove whose dick is bigger, we can talk about why I gathered you here today. Everyone besides Boogie, Tazz, Bentley, Nicky, and Nathan, get out. You can come get your guns when the meeting is over. Jerrod?"

"Yeah, Caesar?" Jerrod asked, trying to mask his anger.

"This isn't going to be like one of those movies where someone in your position crosses me later. You're not always going to like the boss's calls, but you're here to follow them. Am I going to have any problems with you?"

"I'm not happy about none of this shit. Can't even lie on that one," Jerrod grumbled. "But you're my family, and I'm happy you're home, so no, you won't have no issues. But you ain't have to say that shit about my mama."

Jerrod shook his head and exited the basement with the rest of the men. When they were alone, everybody took a seat. Boogie sat in the middle of Tazz and Bentley while Nicky and Nathan sat on opposite sides of Caesar. Nobody said anything for a while until Nicky finally addressed Boogie again.

"I never took you for the soldier type," he said and looked Boogie up and down. "I heard you didn't even want to take over for your old man. Heard you wanted to cook or some shit."

"Things change," Boogie responded.

"Apparently they do. I'd never seen any shit like what you pulled on me. Never seen a block guarded like that . . . nah. I've never seen a single man guarded like that, not even Caesar. And that's saying something. You have potential to be a great leader. Your people believe in you.

You just gotta start using this." Nicky pointed to his head. "And not this." He pointed to his heart. "Emotions start wars. *Thinking* is what keeps the peace."

"You're right. And that's why I'm here. What I did caused a terrible ricochet effect. The Chinese are after us now, and they want blood. We're at war, all of us."

"That's why you called them here, Unc?" Nathan asked and laughed loudly. He looked at Caesar. "Ain't nobody scared of the Chinese. Of the Five Families, they were always the weakest!"

"There are many things I haven't told anybody in my own efforts to keep the peace," Caesar sighed. "But I have to disagree with you, nephew. The Chinese were never the weakest. In fact, they might be stronger than we all think."

Chapter 6

Brrrrrr! Brrrrrr!

The sudden vibration from his phone almost made Marco drop the tools in his hands. He was in the middle of assembling an AR-15 assault rifle in the privacy of his work shed. When he checked it, he didn't recognize the number, which made him curious, because the only people who had his number were people who were supposed to.

"Hello?" he answered.

"Marco," was all the voice said, but instantly he knew who it was.

"Tao."

"You don't sound too happy to hear from me. And that makes me believe that my thoughts about you avoiding me are true," Tao said, making a "tsk" sound a few times with his tongue.

"Avoiding you?" Marco said and placed the gun down on his work desk. "Is that what you think I've been doing?"

"I can't think of any other reason for not hearing from you after my uncle was murdered."

"Other than the fact that I was busy in a war just like you were, you mean," Marco shot back, and he could hear Tao suck his teeth.

"Even still, our families have an alliance. You are to always come to our aid when we are in need."

"Then when were you at when my warehouses were getting bombed? You're not the only one who had casualties, amigo," Marco said. "If this alliance is only good on one side, then what good is it really for me?"

There was silence on the other end, and Marco didn't know what to expect. Behind him there was a knock on the shed, and when he turned around, he saw his son, Lorenzo, poking his head inside. Marco waved him inside and then held up a finger to tell him to wait a second.

"You are right," Tao's voice finally sounded again. "We have failed each other. But there is still time to make things right. I think it is time to bring you over to the big-boy table and let you in on a few things."

"A few things like what?"

"Like how we are going to get rid of this pest problem before it spreads. Please, meet me tonight at my uncle's Chinese restaurant, Dim Sum, at eight o'clock. Fortune is under construction."

"All right, I'll be there," Marco said without hesitation. The phone disconnected, and he picked the gun back up before turning to his son. "Is everything okay, Zo?"

"Yeah," Zo said with a shrug. "I just wanted to come out here and check on you. Every time I've come over to visit you and mama, you're holed up in this shed. You good?"

He sat down in a folding chair beside his father and patted him on the shoulder. Zo was Marco's oldest child and next in line to take over the family business. Zo was 28 and a whole head taller than Marco. He was fit and muscular and had a passion for weaponry just like Marco. He was every father's dream son, and he couldn't be prouder.

"I'm good. Sometimes a man just needs time to clear his head," he told his son.

"Should I be concerned about what needs that much clearing?"

"No, you shouldn't be. Now did you handle that order like I told you to?"

"Yes. Fifty semiautomatic handguns to the Ortiz family. They wired over their payment this morning."

"Perfect. I don't know why I even asked. You always handle business promptly," Mario said.

He had been giving what Diana and Caesar had suggested some thought, about letting the new generation take over the family businesses, but then he put it to the back of his mind. He wasn't ready to step down yet. There was still so much work to do and money to get. Zo might have understood the ins and outs of the money trade for weapons, and he could tell anyone about any gun placed in his hands, but he just wasn't cutthroat enough. He just *cared* too much and had too much mercy in him. It was one of his best qualities, he'd gotten it from his mother, but Marco feared he would be looked at as a pushover. His second child, though, Leticia, was a hard ass just like him. She was only five foot five but walked around like she was twenty feet tall. Guns were her forte as well. As soon as she was out of high school, she joined the family business. If she had her way, she would take over for Marco when he stepped down. But it was Zo who was first in line to receive any title.

"So who was that on the phone?" Zo asked curiously.

"Just a business colleague. He wants to meet and discuss a few things tonight," Marco said and finished putting together the gun. "Nothing you need to worry yourself with."

"And I won't, as long as no more of our warehouses get blown up. It took me weeks to make up for all of that lost inventory. We just got caught back up on orders. And honestly, *Papá,* I think it may be time to take on some new clients."

"Eh." Marco swatted the air with his hand. "Now isn't the time."

"We need the money," Zo told him. "We still have some losses to recuperate from. And we won't be able to do that without new money."

"And we will when we have the time to screen motherfuckers. The process is too extensive. And no dollar is worth it if we accidently sell to a narc or a motherfucker wearing a wire. And right now we can't spare a second on a background check. We do business with who we know, and that's it. Understand? Things will be all right as long as there is a constant flow."

"*Papá,* what do you mean we won't have time? Is there something you aren't telling me? I thought the war was over. I thought you said Boogie came to his senses."

"He did, but on the way, he made a few mistakes. Big ones."

"You mean by killing Li?" Zo asked.

"Yes. And the Chinese are pretty pissed off about it. Li's nephew, Tao, isn't someone whose bad side you want to be on. He's missing a few screws, and the worst part about a crazy motherfucker is you never know what they're gonna do next. Now come, let's go have some lunch before I head over to Caesar's."

"I'll come with you," Zo suggested, and Marco patted him on his arm twice.

"No, we're just gonna be doing old-man shit," he said. "But I do have a job for you if you're up to it."

"Anything."

"I need you to find a new safehouse for all of our dirty money waiting to be cleaned. A place that only you and our most trusted know about. With the Pact gone, I want the other families to know as little about me as possible."

Chapter 7

Tao clicked his tongue against his teeth after he hung up with Marco. He stared at the device for a while. It would have been longer had it not been for the sound of someone clearing their throat. He blinked once and suddenly remembered where he was.

"Oh, right. Where were we?" he asked and smiled sinisterly.

He, four of his henchmen, and his younger brother's bodyguard, Han, were standing inside of his brother Shen's bedroom. Bloody and bound to the bed with their arms over their heads were Shen and a black whore whose name Tao didn't care to know. By the time he was done with her she would just be another Jane Doe. Shen's face was twisted up in anger and beet red. He kept trying to scream, but it just came out as a muffled cry against the duct tape on his mouth. The brown-skinned woman had sweat beads sliding down her forehead and mixing with the tears streaming from her eyes. Terror was written all over her face, and Tao was loving every second of it.

"You know what happens when people betray me, brother. Why would you do something as foolish as plot against me?" Tao asked and snatched the duct tape from Shen's mouth.

"Brother!" Shen gasped. He had a gash above his left eye from where one of the men had punched him, and he was trying to blink away the blood. "Don't do this! It's not what you think."

"Oh, but isn't it? Why else would you be in bed with one of Diana's whores?" Tao asked.

"We've always gotten women from the Sugar Trap. Brother, please."

"Not while we're at war with them! I can't think of one good solid reason why Diana would give you access to one of the girls, unless this is the way you're trying to swap information against me."

"I would never do something like that," Shen insisted. "You're making a mistake."

"No, you're the one who seems to have made the mistake. I always told Uncle you were our weakest link, but he didn't believe me. He believed he could still groom you to be like the rest of us." Tao reached down and snatched the duct tape from the woman's mouth. She flinched at the sharp pain, and her bottom lip quivered when Tao spoke to her. "Do you want to live?"

"Yes," she said.

"Tell me then, why are you here?"

"I . . . I didn't ask for any of this," she said, and more tears came down her face. "I just wanna go home now. Please let me go!"

"I'm going to let you go as soon as you tell me what it is I need to know. Tell me why you're here," Tao repeated and watched the woman look tearfully up at Shen with an apology in her eyes.

"I'm so sorry. But I want to live," she said to him even though he shook his head at her in dread. She ignored it and turned back to Tao. "Boogie sent me."

"Boogie?" Tao made a face.

"Yes. He's been running all of Harlem since Diana has been taking a break. He didn't tell me too much except I was supposed to come here, get some information, and bring it back to him."

"And what information is that?"

"That someone named Chu On Yee is here. That's all I know, I swear. Please let me go!"

She had no idea how much her words made Tao's skin crawl. When Shen's bodyguard called Tao and told him he'd walked in with a girl from the Sugar Trap, he thought he was just being paranoid with his thoughts. In fact, he'd only let his henchmen beat Shen up for the sheer fact alone that he had the enemy's property in his home. Now he wished he'd let them do more.

"Thank you for your information," Tao said to her, his voice low and strangely calmer than before.

"You said you would let me go, remember?" she said weakly.

"I did, didn't I?" Tao walked to her side of the bed and sat down beside her. He reached one hand like he was about to untie her. "Well, let's take care of that, why don't we?"

"Tao, don't," Shen said, but it was too late.

Tao had already pulled a thick knife from the inside of his suit jacket. By the time the woman saw the glimmer of the blade, Tao was plunging it into her chest. She gasped and jerked once, but she was dead in seconds. Tao shook his head in a disappointed fashion as he removed the knife and wiped the blood off of it with the bedspread.

"I truly didn't plan on killing anybody today," Tao said and looked sadly at Shen. "Especially my own brother. Why? Why have you done this to me? You choose the blacks over your own blood? Give me a reason to spare you!"

"I . . . I can't," Shen said. "You said it already. I'm not like you and Uncle. I never will be. I don't want to be the kind of man who steps on everyone just for a piece of power. I don't want to kill people and hurt people."

"Because you're weak."

"No, Tao. It's because I have a soul. Something you sold a long time ago. I want peace, real peace. And the blacks, as you call them, are the ones who can give it! They've already given it!"

Tao scoffed. "They are the reason we are in this war! They broke their own sacred Pact."

"Oh, bullshit, brother. I was there the night Uncle was murdered. I know the truth," Shen said, looking Tao in the eyes and scowling. "I know the truth."

"You know nothing!" Tao sneered, standing back up.

"Answer me this: if I'm a traitor, what does that make you?"

"Enough of this. I won't continue to speak with a man who conspired with the enemy!"

"Too afraid your secret might come out in front of them?" Shen nodded his head toward the other men in the room. "Killing me won't erase who you are, brother."

Tao turned his head and looked at his henchmen and Shen's bodyguard, Han. They seemed uninterested in what Shen was saying. They stood still with their eyes locked on him, awaiting their orders. But Tao didn't want to give the satisfaction of killing Shen to anyone else. He wanted it for himself. The anger inside of him made him numb. So numb that he hardly felt his fingers wrap around his pistol and aim it at his brother's skull. So numb that he barely felt the recoil of the gun when he fired it. He stared at the smoke coming from the bullet hole in Shen's forehead and felt no loss.

"I always wanted to be an only child," he said to the dead body. He looked down at the gun in his hand before glancing up at Han. "Han, come stand where I'm standing."

"Yes, sir." Han did so without question, and Tao moved out of the way.

"Take this," he said and handed him his gun. "Now give me your gun." Once again, Han did so without question. Tao stepped back by the other men and gave them a sudden incredulous look. "So you're going to just stand there after he just killed my brother?"

"Huh? What?" Han's eyes widened, and he looked at the gun in his hand. "Boss, this has to be a joke. *You* just killed your brother."

"And now he's lying about what he's done. Kill him. Now! Or I will have all of your heads!" Tao ordered, and like good dogs, they did as they were told.

When Han saw that they were about to follow his orders, he raised the gun in his hand and shot first. He caught the man closest to Tao in the face and killed him, but that was where his luck ended. The others lit his body up like a Christmas tree at the holidays. His body jerked violently before he dropped dead. The men lowered their guns, thinking that they were safe, but when they turned around to face Tao, they were in for another surprise. They were staring down the barrel of his pistol.

"Sorry, I don't like to leave any loose ends," he said with a shrug.

He fired the gun three times and delivered fatal shots to them. When he was the only one left alive, he looked at the bloodbath around him. After the allegations Shen made against him, there was no way Tao could let any of them leave alive. He couldn't risk any more rebels taking live form or action against him in their own hands. He pulled out his phone and made a phone call.

"Hello, Father?" Ming said when he answered the phone.

"Son! I need you to send cleaners to Uncle Shen's house now!" Tao said in a fake tearful voice.

"Is everything okay?"

"No, it isn't! Your uncle is dead."

"What? No!"

"The blacks killed him. Your uncle called me over here and said something was off about him, but by the time I got here, it was too late. He's dead."

"How?"

"Your uncle, the humanitarian, was trying to offer a peaceful solution. He told me he had met with them and everything seemed fine. They even offered him one of their best whores," Tao lied through his teeth. "But I think they used her to find his home. They killed him and all of his security. Men who worked for us. We have to tighten up everywhere, son. Especially with Chu On here. Do you understand me?"

"Yes, Father," Ming said sadly and grew quiet.

"I will be at the mansion soon. Do what I have asked. Quickly!"

"Yes, Father," Ming repeated, and Tao could hear the sadness in his voice.

Ming had been close to Shen. He would take his death hard, but it was all for his own good. Tao didn't need Shen poisoning his son with weakness. It was already bad enough having him for a brother. He refused to have a traitor for a son. He wanted to make an example of his brother's weak heart and also add fuel to the hatred of the other Families. He looked around again and let out a breath. *What a day.*

Chapter 8

"Ah!" Diana hissed and clutched her stomach.

She had been bending down and trying to reach a pan in a lower cabinet when she felt a sharp pain in her side. It wasn't so bad that she was in excruciating pain, but she definitely needed to catch her breath. Diana tried to be as silent as she could, because she didn't want—

"Diana! I told you to tell me if you needed my help with anything!"

Too late. Morgan had heard her and had rushed into the kitchen to see what was wrong. Diana stood up straight when the pain subsided and waved her hand.

"I am fine. I just bent over wrong, that's all."

"Well, I really don't think you're supposed to be bending at all, let alone trying to cook a whole meal by yourself."

"I can't just sit around and do nothing!" Diana told her, and it was obvious by her tone that she didn't like being chastised like a child. "I just wanted to make us a little gumbo for lunch."

"Resting isn't doing nothing. It's helping to get your body back in tip-top shape. I know you're tired of being cooped up at home." Morgan walked over to Diana and took the pot from her hands. "And as far as the gumbo, how about you talk me through it and I make it?"

"Nobody makes my gumbo like I make it," Diana grumbled but sighed when Morgan shot her a fed-up look. "Fine."

"Yay! We need to spend some mother-daughter bonding time anyways to make up for these twenty-plus years," Morgan said and gave Diana a fond look.

It still amazed her that Morgan wasn't mad at her for keeping a secret that big from her. In fact, her daughter was angrier at her adoptive parents for not ever telling her she was adopted. Ever since Diana had been shot, Morgan had been staying with her. And although she could be a pain, she had to admit she was glad someone was there to help her. She might not have looked her age, but she sure felt it.

"First you need to make your roux. Grab that bowl, and whisk a cup of flour together over the stove with those bacon drippings. It's already measured."

"Okay," Morgan said, smiling, and did as she was told. "You know, my mom, I mean my other mom, never taught me how to cook. She just hated for anybody to be in her kitchen."

"Well, if you had been with me, you would have been cooking all the time."

"Too bad you gave me up," Morgan said absentmindedly, and Diana fell silent. Morgan caught wind of what she had just done and stopped whisking. "No, I'm sorry. That came out completely wrong. I don't want you to think I'm mad at you. I'm not. I'm just . . ." Morgan sighed. "I'm still just working through some things, you know?"

"I know," Diana said.

"I know you did what you had to do to give me a good life, and now that I am a part of yours, I know all of this would have been too chaotic for a small child. God brought me back to you at the right time." She paused briefly. "What was he like? My birth father, I mean."

"Just like Boogie, just a tad bit more cynical," Diana said with a small laugh. "And just like you, smart and adaptable. He would have loved you. I will have to live with the regret of not telling him about you for the rest of my life. I guess I just always thought I had more time."

"How did the two of you fall in love?" Morgan asked, still whisking away.

"The way most young people do," Diana laughed. "One night of forbidden passion was all it took to get that man hooked on me. But I'd be a liar to say I wasn't hooked on him too. One thing I'll say about you is that you were made out of love, because I loved that man deeply. He deserved better than what Dina gave him."

"Both he and Boogie did," Morgan said and shook her head. "That bitch was bat shit crazy. Speaking of Boogie, have you heard from him? I haven't in a few days."

"He's good."

"How do you know that?"

"Because he's out there handling business. He just had a meeting with Caesar."

"So you talked to Caesar, and he told you?"

"No," Diana said with a small smile. "There is so much that I have to teach you. And one of the main things is keeping your ears to the streets. All they do is make noise. And right now they're talking about how foolish Caesar is to have let Boogie back into the fold."

"Yeah, well, let his old ass be foolish in peace!" The voice caught both Diana and Morgan by surprise.

Diana couldn't believe she hadn't heard Boogie walking toward the kitchen let alone enter the home. He had his own key and had been making routine checks on her ever since they left the Big House. He was dressed casually in jeans and a jean jacket, and he had a fresh haircut.

"You know, there is an invention called a phone. Maybe you should use it before you just pop up." Diana put her hand on her hip in frustration.

"What fun would that be?" he asked and kissed her on the cheek.

"I think she just has a little PTSD after getting shot," Morgan teased.

"And you're both going to have PTSD after I put my foot in both your asses," Diana warned and pointed at a plate of vegetables. "Put those in the food processor, Morgan. After that, boil your beef bouillon cubes."

"Okay."

"What are y'all making?" Boogie asked, looking at the food on the counter.

"Gumbo. You gonna stay and eat?" Morgan asked, looking over her shoulder.

"Free food? You already know!"

"Good." Morgan grinned.

Diana grabbed a bottle of brandy from a glass cabinet and poured two shots. She pointed for Boogie to sit at the island beside her while Morgan cooked. After she handed him one of the shots, they both tapped them on the island and threw them back. Diana's went down smooth, but Boogie hissed when the burning sensation hit his chest.

"That's going to put some hair on your chest," she told him.

"Nah, I don't think Roz would go for that," Boogie said, talking about his girlfriend.

"How is she and her daughter?"

"Good," Boogie said, and then his face grew hard. "I have a round-the-clock watch on them."

"As you should. It's too crazy not to."

"Yeah, even Caesar's worried."

"What did he say? Tell me about the meeting. How did it go?"

"Before or after Nathan had a gun pointed at my head?"

"His crazy ass," Diana chuckled. "He's a great one to have at your side. Terrible to have as an enemy."

"I can see that. After he calmed down and they got used to my presence, we talked. And Caesar feels that the Chinese are a bigger threat than what we think."

"Why?"

"He didn't say," Boogie said and stared at the island deep in thought. "What did you know about Li?"

"Li? He was cunning. The type of person who hid in plain sight. His father was the last one brought to the table, you know? He and Caesar had been fighting. Li's father wanted to take over the drug exchange in New York."

"Really?" Boogie asked. That was news to him.

"Yeah, this was a lifetime ago. But he did. However, New York could only have one drug kingpin, and Caesar went to war over that title. He died shortly after that, and I guess when Li took over, he figured the wise thing would be to join us rather than feud. Still, Li's presence was always just business. That's it. He never felt like family."

"How could Caesar ever trust him if he knew Li wanted what he had?"

"You've heard the phrase 'keep your friends close but your enemies closer'? There is always a method behind Caesar's madness," Diana said and took another shot. "How are my streets looking?"

"Good. Money has been a constant, no girl has fallen out of line, and all have paid their dues on time. They're wondering when you're gon' be back at the Sugar Trap though."

"Are there any issues I should know about?"

"No."

"Then I'll be back when I good and damn well please," Diana said.

She knew taking over for her had been a lot to ask of him, especially since he was busy handling his own business, but he proved to be a tycoon, and he didn't complain once. Boogie was more of a blessing than even he knew. He might have had a lot of people who hated him, but there were those who still loved him. She was one of them.

"Well, take all the time you need. I don't mind keepin' busy. Plus I got some help. Bentley been movin' around to the places I can't. I'ma need him to go speak to the Italians soon. Most of them left, but the ones who stayed aren't feelin' our movement on the Island since we killed Bosco."

"You just have to be smart and watch your back on all ends."

"Hell yeah. I feel like everybody wants my head on a stick because of the things I've done."

"Baby, no matter what you do, people will want your head on a stick. It comes with having the thing that everybody wants—power," Diana said and hit him softly on the chest. "Now let me go help this girl before she ruins our dinner!"

Chapter 9

Being unpredictable was any great man's strength, but when it was the strength of an opponent, it became a nuisance. Caesar sat in his study staring at a small table in front of him. On that table was a chessboard, and all of the pieces were in their beginning places. As he puffed away at his cigar, he couldn't help but to wonder what Tao's next move was going to be. Through Marco, Caesar had come to know that Tao was a ruthless son of a bitch, but he was smart. He had tested Caesar's temperature, and now that he knew how hot it was, Caesar suspected him to come harder the next time around.

The sound of someone clearing their throat jarred him from his thoughts. He looked up and saw the middle-aged housekeeper standing there with Marco.

"I'm sorry to disturb you, Mr. King, but you have a visitor," she said sweetly.

"Thank you, Tabitha. You can leave us," he told her.

She left, and Marco took a seat in a chair near him. Caesar had been expecting him ever since he called and told him that Tao wanted to meet that evening. He offered Marco a cigar, which he politely declined. However, when he offered him a glass of scotch, he took it without a second thought. He poured himself a glass too and took a sip before placing it on a coaster beside the chessboard.

"You still do that?" Marco asked and chuckled.

"Do what exactly?"

"Stare at the game instead of play it."

"I guess so," Caesar said and smiled at his own expense. "It's something that I apply to my life as well. I sit back and watch as the game unfolds before I decide to make my move."

"And what's your move?"

"I don't know. I'm still watching." Caesar rubbed his chin. "So that motherfucka wants to meet you tonight, huh? What do you think he wants?"

"I don't know. Probably to kill you," Marco said bluntly. "And he wants me to help him do it."

"When Tao was alive, did he ever mention coming after me?"

"No. He always made it seem like if the two of you fought, he would be defending himself. But then again, Li might not have truly trusted that my allegiance was to him. He might not have told me at all."

"You're probably right. These months of having you spy on Li, I never thought to have you watch Tao. I don't know anything about him, or how he moves. I'm losing my touch."

"Well, amigo, I've learned enough," Marco said, taking a swig of his drink and then hissing as it went down. "And what I can tell you is as good as that *vato* is making it look, he doesn't give a damn about Li's body rotting in the ground. And I don't blame him, Li talked to everyone around him like they were beneath him, blood or not. I'm surprised none of them made him kick the bucket sooner."

"If any of them wanted to, they couldn't. Li was protected."

"Protected by the Pact?"

"Not just the Pact, I'm afraid," Caesar said and put the cigar out. "Have I ever told you the story of how Li became part of our union?"

"You beat his father in a war," Marco said and shrugged.

"No." Caesar shook his head. "I beat him in a battle, but he could have won the war."

"I don't get it, amigo."

"Before he died, my father used to always tell me one thing: watch the Asians, because they're always watching you."

"Was your old man racist?" Marco joked, but Caesar didn't laugh.

"No, he wasn't. He was a smart man. And one thing smart men do is ask questions. You never wondered how a Chinese family could come here from China and become one of the wealthiest families in the state? Hell, have you ever wondered how a Chinese family could come and take over a main borough like the Bronx?"

"I . . . I guess not. They've been there since I was a kid, so I never wondered where they came from."

"Don't worry about it. I'll tell you, my good friend. It's because they already had the money, the status, and the power before they got here. They already had the soldiers and the firepower. And who do you know in China who has all of that?"

Caesar watched as the realization spread on Marco's face. Soon after was a look of disbelief, but then the reality set in again.

"The Triad," Marco finally spoke.

"Yes. Li's father died in his sleep before he could continue feuding with me. I won by a miraculous default. But even after, I didn't trust Li when he came into power, which is why I urged him to agree to the Pact instead of war. The truth is, I didn't think we would really win the war. Even with the other families backing me. There would have been nothing but senseless death and barely anything left of New York to rule. I also knew that as long as the Pact was in place, the Chinese would abide. Their honor is something that they don't take lightly. Which is why I think it's too dangerous for you to go meet Tao tonight. If they find out you've been playing both sides, they'll kill you."

"I have to. It's the only way for us to know what the hell they're planning to do, amigo," Marco told him. "And right now, I'm the only one with a way in. I wanna use it."

"Marco . . ."

"You know I'm right."

"I know. I just wish you weren't."

Caesar didn't want to agree, but he had to.

Chapter 10

The calming sound of running water hit Marco's ears when he entered the Chinese establishment. There was a beautiful water fountain with many coins inside stationed by the front double doors. In the distance, families of all colors and sizes were enjoying a nice dinner out in the dining room. With Marco were two of his best shooters, Duan and Pedro. Upon seeing them, a very pretty Chinese woman wearing a black and red kimono approached.

"Tao is waiting for you," she said with a strong accent. "This way please."

She led them up a flight of stairs to the second level of the restaurant to an office area, where Tao was waiting for him with his own muscle standing around him. He sat behind a thick wooden desk that was facing the door Marco had walked through.

"The man of the hour is finally here," Tao said, standing up and holding out a hand. "I know you were used to meeting my uncle at Fortune, but as you know, it's under construction."

He spoke lightheartedly, but Marco knew better. Fortune was the restaurant Boogie had gotten blown up. It was the explosion that had killed Li. Marco shook his hand and gave it a firm squeeze. The two men stared each other down until something else caught Marco's attention. It was on the collar of Tao's white button-up underneath his suit jacket.

"You've got a little something right here," Marco said and pointed at his own collar when he pulled his hand away. "Is it blood?"

"Probably," Tao said nonchalantly. "I've had a long day. I'm sure you've had a few of those."

"Sure," Marco said.

"Sit. I have a few things that I would like to discuss with you," Tao said and pointed at the chair behind Marco.

Marco plopped down in the seat across from him with Duan and Pedro close behind him. He could tell that Tao was sizing him up, so he wore his best poker face. He didn't know Tao, but he knew that the energy he carried made the hairs on the back of his neck stand up.

"Let's skip the small talk, shall we? I just want to jump right into it. I'm not one who likes to waste time," Tao started and brought his hands together, touching only at the fingertips. "The agreement that you had with my uncle?"

"What about it?"

"What good is it to me?"

Tao's question threw Marco completely off. "Excuse me?"

"What good is it to me? The agreement," Tao repeated.

"Need I remind you that it was your uncle who came to me in the first place about any kind of partnership," Marco said.

"Because he thought he needed you."

"And you're saying that you don't need me?"

"I'm asking you to give me a reason to."

"Well, for starters, it doesn't seem like you have too many friends right now," Marco said, playing his role.

"Which is crazy when you really think about it, right? We get attacked, and the other families side with our attackers. So who really is the enemy?" Tao asked with a raised brow.

"I can empathize. I lost a lot of money behind that . . . What should I call it? Temper tantrum."

"Yet, your loyalty still lies with Caesar." It came out as a statement, but Marco knew that Tao was just testing him.

"My loyalty lies with my family and whatever is the greater good for them," he answered with a straight face.

"So would I be able to trust you?"

"You would be able to trust me as much as I would be able to trust you. So you tell me," Marco said and saw Tao's eye twitch slightly in annoyance. "I'll be the first to tell you that I didn't come here for a job interview."

"You're correct. You came here because it's time to pick a side," Tao said and leaned forward in his seat. "Now that I am in charge, I am going to rain blood down on anyone who opposes me. And I'm not going to stop until I get what I want."

"And that is?"

"Everything. My uncle was a powerful man, but he was stupid. He should have finished the job his father started and wiped the other Families out, but he thought it would be better to wait. Well, we've waited long enough. Now is the time to show every borough how strong the Triad is."

"The Triad is here?" Marco asked, raising a brow in alarm.

"Yes. Now that you know that, it brings me to the next and most important part in our conversation. My demands."

"Demands?" Marco chuckled. "All right, I'll humor you. Just for fun. What demands do you have?"

"You are to stop providing weapons to the other boroughs and only supply to me."

He'd said it, so of course he was serious. Still, Marco had to repeat the request over and over in his head. Tao had to understand how crazy what he wanted was.

"Mmm, nope. Can't do that," Marco said.

"It wasn't a question," Tao said icily, but Marco wasn't intimidated.

"As I said earlier, I will always look out for the best interest of my family. And what you want isn't in the best interest of them. You seem to want to have the better end of an agreement between us. If I cut off supply to them, I won't make anywhere near the profit I'm making now. Even if you pay double. Plus, Caesar King is and has always been one of my biggest customers."

"He won't be once you cut him off."

"As I said before, I can't do that."

"You can and you will," Tao told him.

"How would that benefit me?"

"It will benefit you because you'll get to keep your life. Tell me, Marco, how much is that worth to you?"

"Are you threatening me, Tao?"

"I'm just telling you that if you don't want to join me completely with no ties to them, then I have no use for you. Li used you to get information about Caesar, but sitting across from you, I don't think I would trust anything you say."

"And why is that?"

"You say you aren't loyal to Caesar *or* to us, yet you still formed an alliance with my uncle. Why is that?"

"Playing it safe," Marco said with a shrug.

"Or it could be that you are playing both sides," Tao said and studied Marco's face. Marco tried to stay as blank as possible and didn't breathe until Tao blinked. "You could be, and how would I know until it's too late? It would have been very convenient to have you in the fold, but why ask for what I can just take? Sometimes you have to cut off your finger to save your hand."

He made a tiny hand gesture, and Marco felt like he was dismissing him.

"If you think I'm the finger you're talking about, you have another think coming." Marco chuckled again. "It's time for me to leave. Thank you for your time."

"Oh, you must not understand." Tao faked a look of concern. "The only way you're leaving is in a bag."

"And you must not understand that my men are prepared to fight to the death to get me out of here."

"I don't know about the fight part, but death seems fitting for them," Tao told him.

He was staring at something behind Marco and had an eerie look in his eyes. There was something about the pleasured smile on his lips. It was sadistic and made Marco turn around in his seat. And once he did, he wished he hadn't. Both of his big and muscular guards were being held from behind with hands over their mouths and slit throats. Marco hadn't heard a sound behind him and didn't know how Tao's men had moved with so much stealth. Duan and Pedro were still standing upright while the blood from their necks poured onto their clothes. As Marco watched in horror, Tao's men let their lifeless bodies fall to the floor.

"Duan . . . Pedro," he said in a barely audible voice. Suddenly he remembered the hand gesture Tao made. It hadn't been an order to dismiss him. It was a kill order. He turned back to Tao and glared at him. "You . . ."

"My men are trained in ninja warfare. They are able to move without making a sound or alerting an enemy to their presence. So imagine the power of the Triad. Any last words?"

It was then that the fear set in. Not of Tao, but because Marco knew he wasn't making it out of there alive. He would never see his children again or tell his wife that he loved her. He hadn't even gotten to say goodbye. Their faces were running through his head like a rerun, and he hoped they would be okay without him.

"Yeah, fuck you. You piece of shit," Marco spat out right as his gun was snatched from his waist and a plastic bag was placed over his head.

Chapter 11

Becoming one with the shadows was one of Ming's greatest strengths. A person wouldn't know he was there until he made his presence obvious. It made stalking his prey easy. When he was just a boy, his father had sent him away to China to learn the ways of the Triad. He was trained in ninja arts to become the ultimate soldier. He had no attachments to worldly possessions. The only thing he lived for was to be loyal to his family. That was why he was still reeling over his uncle's death.

Growing up, Shen had been Ming's only escape from his father's horrible punishments when he made small mistakes. And when he became an adult, the love Shen showed him continued. He believed Ming was more than just the soulless killer Tao had created.

"You are a person, not an object someone can turn on and off. Remember that."

His uncle's voice and sayings had played in his head many times after Ming found out about his murder. But they quieted when Ming saw the nature in which he had died. It was a savage and unforgiveable crime. What he planned to do to the people responsible was unthinkable and inhumane. That was why he couldn't allow his uncle's voice to talk him out of unleashing his rage.

Ming wasn't a man who needed an army of men around him to make a move on any enemy. In fact, he preferred to be alone with just him, his gun, and his kunai knives. He moved through the streets of Brooklyn and Harlem undetected as he followed Boogie and his cronies around. He got a sense of what Boogie's day was like and took note that he spent more time in Harlem than in his own territory. In fact, Ming waited in the parking lot of the Sugar Trap for a long time. He watched patiently as the bouncers IDed and patted down men before letting them enter the club. He also saw them get rough with a few patrons who were belligerently drunk. Ming checked the clock on his car and saw that it was nearing midnight. A part of him told himself that he was just there to gather information, but another part knew that if he saw a window of opportunity to kill Boogie, he would take it. No hesitation.

Thirty minutes later, the bouncers opened the doors again to let someone out, and finally Ming saw Boogie exit. He wasn't alone. Two men stood on either side of him, cautiously checking their surroundings. Ming smirked. They knew times were dangerous, even on their own turf. He watched as they walked Boogie to an awaiting SUV, and then he got inside. Only one of the men he was with got in and drove off with him. When they were gone, the remaining man glanced back at the Sugar Trap as if he wanted to go back inside, but then he shook his head. He began to walk toward the back of the parking lot where Ming was parked.

The man pulled out a set of keys, and when he pressed a button, an Audi's lights flashed. The SUV was parked diagonally from Ming's car, away from the security of overhead lights. Ming pulled over his head a mask with the eyes cut out. Quietly, he got out of his car and shut the door. His feet made no noise as he moved in the shadows of the night and approached the Audi.

"It's always, 'Gino grab this, Gino grab that,'" the man was mumbling to himself when he finally got to his vehicle. "Them niggas gon' really need me one day, and I'm not gon' answer the . . . Ay! What the fuck?"

Ming had sprung from the shadows and kicked him in the back of the knee to make him lose balance. Before he fell to his knees, Ming wrapped a strong arm around his neck. In all of his trainings, Ming was taught to make all of his kills as quick as possible and with little to no verbal exchange. The man tried to speak, but his words came out in a gurgle. Ming grabbed one of the knives from his belt, holding it with a firm grip.

"This is for my uncle," Ming breathed into the side of the man's face and shoved the kunai through the side of his neck.

He didn't know how important the man was to Boogie, but finding him dead with the knife lodged into his neck would send a message. He released the man and let him fall to the ground while a pool of blood formed around him. His death didn't make Ming feel better. All it did was make him thirstier for blood. And it was then that he knew he wouldn't stop until it was Boogie who was laid out in front of him, dead.

Chapter 12

Normally Tao didn't feel any kind of way after killing a man. And when he had murdered Marco, that fact still remained. However, murdering his own brother had started to take a toll on him. At first he was fine and unbothered. But the night that followed was riddled with nothing but nightmares. Tao knew he had to cleanse his body and clear his mind if he was going to get past it. The best way to do that was at their family-owned massage parlor in the Opulent Suite. It was the only part of the whole parlor that offered happy endings.

"Hsss, ahhh!" Tao moaned with his head back.

He was sitting in a comfortable chair as delicate hands belonging to a beautiful Chinese woman massaged his feet with warm oil. While she did that, another Chinese woman massaged his manhood with her throat. Tao's hand was on the back of her head as it bobbed up and down his shaft, and he gasped at the double dose of pleasure. Both women were naked and doing their jobs making him a very happy man. Shen was pushed to the back of his mind as he felt his climax building up. When finally he exploded in her mouth, a loud moan escaped his lips. The blissful sensation lasted a total of ten seconds, and when it was gone, he yanked the woman's head up by her hair and dismissed her with a wave.

"You stay," he instructed the woman massaging his feet when she made to follow after the other. "Keep doing that until I tell you to stop."

She nodded her head without saying anything and kept pressing her thumbs into the soles of his feet. Tao re-wrapped the towel around his waist, leaned back into the chair again, and closed his eyes. Just when he thought he was rid of the thoughts of Shen, they began to plague him again. His final words played over and over in Tao's head.

"I know the truth."

Shen had spoken the words with confidence, but he couldn't have known what he was talking about. He couldn't have. Nobody was present when he made the phone call to Boogie and told him where Li was going to be that night. Boogie himself didn't even know who made the call. Things had turned out better than Tao could have ever planned.

The night that Li was killed, he was meeting with members of the Triad about their involvement in Li's business. They had never been happy with his decision to limit himself to just one small corner of an entire state, but they allowed it due to Chu On being his grandfather. However, their patience had worn thin since Chu On was getting too old and it was time for him to name Li as his heir.

Tao saw it as the perfect opportunity to stir the pot and advance himself. When he set up Li's murder, the members of the Triad who were inside Fortune were killed too. Which, as anyone could guess, didn't sit too well with the rest of them. It was the reason why Chu On had left China for the first time in twenty years to come to New York and help eradicate the problem. Tao planned on using it as his opportunity to show his great-grandfather that he was fit to be leader. That was why news of what he had done could never get back to his camp. It was treason and punishable by the harshest form of death. He had done all the work to make sure that there was no dirt on his hands, or so he thought. He didn't know who all Shen had told, but then again Shen could have just been talking. Either way, he planned to keep his eyes in all directions.

In other news, he would have to figure out a way to get more weapons. He had to admit to himself that killing Marco had been a hasty thing to do. He hadn't thought that one all the way through. He'd let the frustration from the day get to him, and when Marco told him no, it flipped a switch inside of him. No matter. He would find a way to get the guns needed to take Caesar, Diana, and Boogie out.

As the woman giving him his massage began to massage his shins and calves with hot stones, a tall black man with a freshly cut beard entered the Opulent Suite. The top of his head was bald, and he had caramel skin. He too had a white towel wrapped around his waist, exposing the hair that looked like ground beef on his muscular chest.

When the man sat in the seat next to Tao, his security made like they were going to make a move toward them. Tao was the only person of interest in the Opulent Suite, and there was an array of security around them, which meant that Tao was the person they were protecting. Tao put a hand up to stop them. He was intrigued that the man was bold enough to take the seat.

"Can I help you?" Tao asked.

"Yes. If you would be so kind as to have one of those women come and give me a massage like you're getting, that would be great," the man said with a smile. "Tao, right?"

The man knowing his name let Tao know that him sitting there was no mistake. The man's face wasn't familiar to him in the slightest. Tao glanced at the man's hand with a bored expression, not having any intention of shaking it. He went back to focusing on the woman doing his massage, but he directed his words at the man.

"I'm not too fond of people knowing who I am when I don't know at all who they are. It would do you some good to introduce yourself to me right now before I let my security take care of you."

"Would they do that with guns or with knives? In my mind I always thought the Triad were a bunch of bad-ass ninjas."

Those words made Tao wave away the woman massaging him and sit up and face the man next to him. He eyed him down, taking in his image, and he was sure he didn't recognize him at all. He had never seen him in New York before, but somehow he knew about the Triad. Who was he?

"Do you work for Caesar?" Tao asked, and the man scoffed.

"I don't work for anybody but myself."

"Then I assume that you have come here for a reason. Other than subtly telling me that you've been watching me."

"Your assumption is correct. I'm here with you because I believe we have a common interest."

"And what might that be?"

"Killing a nigga named Bryshon Toliver. I believe he goes by Boogie."

"And why do you want to do that?"

"I have a bone to pick with him. He caused quite the rumble in my house. In fact, he has left me with no immediate family. And I don't like that."

"Who are you?"

"My name is Simon Hafford. Boogie killed my older brother, Shamar, and my nephew, Shane."

"Shane and Shamar?" Tao asked, trying to put his finger on why those names sounded so familiar, and then it clicked. "Those are the names of the men who were trying to step on Caesar's toes. They caused quite the uproar."

"That's neither here nor there with me. All I know is when he killed them, everything in Ohio went to shit. With no one to preside over the drug game, everybody thinks they're a king. It's pure chaos, and I want no part in that."

"Then what do you want?"

"New scenery," he said and then smiled slyly. "And a piece of an even bigger pie."

"And what are you telling me this for?"

"Because I believe we can help each other out to reach a common goal. I can provide you weapons and the skin color you need to move in the enemy's territory. No offense, but I can almost guarantee almost every Asian motherfucka is getting side-eyed in Brooklyn right now. But niggas are common over here in the Bronx. They probably have eyes on you right now and you don't even know it. Let's even the playing field."

His offer of providing weapons was what Tao homed in on. It was like a silver beacon of hope had flown in on a magic carpet. He would have to do some research on this Simon Hafford, but with Marco dead, it might prove to be a good business move . . . if he checked out, anyway.

"If I do allow you to provide my people guns and weapons, what will you ask of me? I'm sure this offer is not just an act of kindness. I know you want something in return."

"See, I've never been like my brother. I've never thought so big. Because you are big motherfuckers everybody seems to come after. If I provide you everything that you need? When you have the controlling interest of all of New York, I just want to rule a small corner of it. Something to call my own, you know? I want to make money in peace and be remembered as the man who helped the king win the throne."

"That's all?"

"That's all. Honestly the satisfaction of killing Boogie means more to me than all of that shit."

"If you want to join forces, Simon Hafford, then you know what you need to do."

"And that is?"

"Prove yourself to me," Tao said, looking Simon directly in the eyes.

"And here I am thinking you were going to ask me to do something hard."

Chapter 13

It wasn't hard for Tao to find his son when he got home. He always knew where Ming was going to be: outside in the garden by the stone fountain. It was where he found peace and meditated. From a distance, Tao watched Ming closely. His eyes were shut, and his body was relaxed. His chest went up and down slowly as he took deep breaths and became one with his surroundings. Slowly, Tao began moving toward him. He made sure to be as quiet as possible so as not to alert Ming of his presence. When he got close enough, he raised a hand and prepared to strike, but when he forcefully brought it down, Ming blocked it effortlessly.

"Father, I thought I had passed all of your tests," he said with his eyes still closed.

"I was just making sure that your senses were still sharp. Did you do what I asked of you?"

"Yes, I disposed of Marco's body."

"Perfect. And as far as those sharp senses of yours? You are going to need them."

"You have a job for me?" Ming opened his eyes.

"There is a man here by the name of Simon Hafford who has come here to New York. His claim is that he wants the same thing I do—to take out Caesar and Boogie. He has his own reasons, but I don't know if I trust him. But if he is telling the truth, it will be good to have someone who looks like *them* on our side."

"You want me to babysit him?" Ming read between the lines.

"In the simplest terms, yes. Do you question me?"

"No, Father."

"Good. Because he is out front waiting for you. Call if there are any problems or if you find out anything."

Ming hesitated before standing. Tao could tell that he wanted to say something, but instead he held his tongue. It was probably better for him that way. He went back inside of the house, leaving his father outside. Tao decided to walk around the house instead of through it to get to the backyard. It gave him time to gather his thoughts. His grandfather, Chu On, was waiting for him by the pond in the backyard.

Tao approached the calming waters of the pond in his backyard. He was fully dressed in his business attire, prepared to tackle the day, but first he needed to talk to his grandfather. Chi On Li wasn't just that, however. He was also one of the leaders of the Triad. It had been twenty years since he'd left Hong Kong, but upon hearing about Li's death, he made it his business to fly to New York as soon as he could. He was sitting on a bench under a tree. Despite being a guest in his great-grandson's home, he had ten men wearing black suits standing around him. Chu On, once a man of great strength and power, was now a small old man in his eighties. His face was wrinkled, and he wore his long white hair in a monk braid. Tao bowed to him when he got to the bench and sat beside him.

"Great-grandfather, I apologize that I was not here to greet you when you arrived." Tao spoke pleasantly, but the old man didn't say a word. Tao cleared his throat and tried again. "I hope that the accommodations are to your liking."

"They will do." Chu On finally spoke in a soft, raspy voice.

"If there is anything—"

"You are nothing like Li," Chu On said, suddenly cutting him off. "My grandson wasn't this incompetent. If he were still alive, the situation would've been handled by now."

"Grandfather, I assure you that we are doing everything in our power to eradicate the problem."

"Then how did your brother end up dead?" Chu On asked, at last looking at Tao.

At the mention of Shen, Tao felt his eye twitch. He could feel Chu On searching his entire demeanor, so he put on his best somber face. Clenching his teeth, Tao glanced at the water sadly and then back at his great-grandfather.

"That is something I will blame myself for until the day I die," Tao said, looking into his eyes. "The blacks killed Shen under my watch. He was a good man, a smart one, too. Sometimes too smart for his own good. But they got him. Our enemies are powerful. And not only that, but they have joined forces together. Before you arrived, things were chaotic. Uncle is dead and now Shen."

"And what's going to change now that I'm here?"

"We'll have the forces to defeat them."

"And what makes you think I'm going to help you?"

"We should have taken New York block by block years ago. Am I wrong to assume that you were going to assist my uncle with acquiring more territory in New York before he died? That is what you sent the Triad here to discuss?"

"It is."

"Then why am I so different if we are in agreement that this small corner of the world we have to settle for is not enough? It was never enough."

"I just refuse to waste my men or my money on a losing battle. I will not waste my drugs by giving them to you in a market that you cannot sell them in. No."

"Then I guess it's a good thing that we are not going to lose. And It's a good thing that Caesar King will be dead soon."

Chu On grunted. In all reality, Tai had only met his grandfather a few times when he was younger. None of those times had been pleasant. He had always felt like Chu On didn't like him very much mostly because he didn't bother to hide the distaste from his face when he looked at Tao. It wasn't a secret that he wasn't too fond of Tao's father, and when he died, it was like he never existed to him. Li had always been his favorite up until the day he died. He was the only person Chu On had even considered to take over for him. Unfortunately for Chu On, Li never had children, so he was looking at the last of his direct bloodline.

"Fine. I will give you the manpower you need to do what needs to be done. But if you do not come out victorious, you will be forfeiting your right to take my place when I am no longer here."

"There's no doubt in my mind that I will come out victorious, and there's no doubt in my mind that I one day will be the leader of the Triad."

"I hope not, because then you'll be answering to your son."

Once the last word was out of his mouth, Chu On stood up from the bench slowly and began to walk away. Instantly the men guarding him circled around him as he walked. Tao watched him walk away and tried to hide the disdain in his eyes. The good thing was he would have the manpower he needed to go directly at Caesar King and Boogie. Killing Marco had been child's play to get under their skin and show them that he was not afraid to go to great lengths to do what needed to be done. He wanted to let them know that none of them were safe.

Chapter 14

"Wake up, Sleeping Beauty," Boogie said and slapped the bottom of Bentley's Timberland.

Bentley had passed out on Boogie's couch when they got in at one in the morning. Normally he would have gone home, but he was just too tired. Boogie hit his shoe again and made his way to the kitchen, where his girlfriend, Roz, had just gotten done with breakfast.

"I haven't seen my brother that worn out since he used to work the block," she commented, looking at Bentley, who was still sleeping with his mouth wide open. "And are those last night's clothes?"

"We had a long day yesterday," Boogie said, snagging a piece of bacon. "It's been a long week actually."

"I still can't believe Caesar is alive. You see they announced it on the news?"

"Nah, I haven't watched much TV lately. What they say?"

"They said . . . Aht! Get a plate." She popped his hand and made a face at him.

"My bad, baby." Boogie grinned and went for the cabinet.

"Boy, you better get a paper plate, because I do not feel like doing any dishes other than these pots or pans. Here."

"Fine, Miss Mean Girl," Boogie teased. He took the plate and began loading it up with French toast, eggs, and bacon. "Okay, now what did they say on the news?"

"That they had made some sort of freak mistake by assuming the body was his. But what they don't understand is why he waited so long to come out and say he was alive."

"The streets know," Boogie said, grabbing a fork and going to sit down at the dining room table.

Roz made her plate and followed. She sat across from Boogie and eyed him down. He could feel her gaze burning a hole in his forehead, but he ignored her. Or he tried to anyways. But if Roz wanted your attention, she was going to get it one way or another.

"What?" He finally looked up at her.

"You think I ain't noticed the fact that you doubled up security on the block? You ain't slick havin' them niggas posted up the street either. You're worried about something. What is it? I thought the noise died down after your mom died, who I'm still glad I didn't get to meet by the way."

"Shit's cool," Boogie lied through his teeth. "But it's not died down all the way. I just want to be cautious. I made a lot of mistakes and hurt a lot of people. Some understand the rules of the game, but others want to make their own."

"Are me and Amber good?" Roz asked with concern in her voice and eyes.

Boogie reached across the table and grabbed her hands in his. He rubbed them with his thumbs and tried to send some reassurance through his touch.

"As long as I'm breathing, you and baby girl gon' be safe. And I plan on being around for a long time. Understand me?"

"You better be. Yo' ass made me fall in love with you and shit." Roz jerked her neck and pointed her fork at him. "Don't play with me, Boogie."

"I'm not playing with you, girl," Boogie said and kissed her knuckles. "And I think it was you who made me fall in love with you. I think you got some voodoo in that pussy or something."

"I'll beat your ass," Roz said, laughing. "Don't say I have voodoo pussy."

"You got to have something, 'cause I'll bleed the streets behind you, girl."

Her smile went from ear to ear. Boogie loved being able to do that. She was such a beautiful woman inside and out. He didn't know what he had done for her to have been brought into his life. Whenever he was in the field, all he thought about was making it home to her and their daughter, Amber. And that thought alone ensured he always would. He would never disappoint them. He especially would never put Amber in the position to be parentless. It was what he was going through, and it was something that he hadn't dealt with. But he knew that when he took the time to finally sit with it, it was going to hit him like a ton of bricks.

At that moment, he heard the sound of a baby panting. He glanced down the hallway, and sure enough, he saw Amber crawling in her pink sleeper toward where she smelled food. Her eyes were still puffy since she'd just woken up, and her hair was all over her head. He watched, amused as she started toward the kitchen but stopped when she saw Bentley asleep on the couch. Her excitement could be felt throughout the house, and she crawled as fast as she could toward him. Boogie almost got up to get her when she pulled herself up on the couch and raised a hand to smack Bentley. The girl didn't know her strength, but Boogie thought better of it. A thunderclap from Amber was just what Bentley needed to finally wake up.

Slap!

"I'm up, damn! I'm . . ." Bentley sprang to life and sat upright, prepared to curse somebody out. But when he saw Amber standing there cracking up, his face instantly softened, and he swooped her up. "Uncle's baby! Was that you who slapped me? Girl, I thought you was a grown man!"

He tickled her until her squeals became breathless, and he let her get some air in her lungs. He hugged her and kissed her cheeks. Amber was the only girl Boogie had ever seen Bentley have a soft spot for besides Roz. If he didn't love anybody else, he loved them.

"Finally you're back in the land of the living." Boogie grinned.

"Man, fuck you. Both of y'all. Y'all know you seen her over here about to slap the black off me."

"And did," Roz laughed. "It wasn't nothin' but a love tap."

"Love tap my ass. Y'all better put this girl in boxing. I'ma probably have a black eye," Bentley said, wiping a hand down his face and sniffing the air. "You cooked, sis?"

"Yeah, give her here and make you a plate," she said and held her arms out.

Bentley brought her the baby and went to wash his hands. After he was done doing that and making his plate, he joined the rest of them at the dining room table. Boogie gave him a look that Bentley recognized, and he nodded. They had business to discuss, but Boogie would wait until Roz was gone. Fortunately for him, Roz was no fool. She rolled her eyes and gathered her food.

"Come on, baby girl. The boys don't want us around. They have stuff to talk about," she said, and when Boogie opened his mouth to say something, she winked. "It's all right, boo. Just come find me before y'all leave."

"Will do," Boogie said and watched her ass jiggle in her plaid pajama pants as she walked away.

"Nigga, I am right here, you know that? And that's my sister," Bentley said, making a face.

"My bad." Boogie smiled sheepishly. "That's my shorty though."

"Whatever. What's the word though? You heard from that nigga Gino?" Bentley asked, stuffing his mouth with French toast.

"Nah. He was supposed to call me this morning and let me know where he wanted to meet to drop off that package."

"His ass probably went back inside the Sugar Trap to get his dick wet when we left."

"Probably. I'm sure he's gon' be calling soon though. Because we'll be needing those explosives."

"Word." Bentley nodded. "On to other shit though—the Italians. What we gon' do about 'em? I know they ain't feelin' us settin' up shop all around the Island. They killed Li'l Freddy and his whole crew last week, man. I don't want no more bodies racking up."

"Me either. We have to come to a common ground with them before the Chinese do," Boogie said with a sigh. "Fighting two wars at the same time just isn't what I'm tryin'a do."

"I feel you. So what do you want me to do? Go down there and lay down the law?"

"Nah, I tried that. It just made shit worse. We need to offer them something."

"Like what? Money? Positions of power?"

"Both," Boogie said. "Make them feel important, valued."

"I like how you think. I'll get a crew together and be right on it," Bentley said and tried to finish scarfing down his food. As he was eating, he felt Boogie's eyes still on him. "Somethin' else on your mind?"

"Yeah, there is actually," Boogie said, rubbing his chin. "I gotta tell you somethin'."

"A'ight, what?"

"It's about the night Li was killed."

"What about it?"

"I never told you how I knew Li was gon' be at Fortune at the exact time he pulled up."

"I thought you said it was a known fact that Li went there often around that time."

"But I personally didn't know that before . . ."

"Before what?"

"I got a tip and a random phone call from somebody I didn't know. And when I play the voice back in my head, I still don't recognize it."

"What did they say?"

"They tipped me off about Li, about where he would be and when. I guess back then I was so blinded by rage that I didn't care who the information was from, just that I got it. I hadn't thought about it again until recently when . . ." He let his voice trail off. "Anyways, somebody else wanted Li dead."

"Damn."

"I don't know who though."

"I would rather know who all my enemies are than have a ghost after me," Bentley said, and Boogie agreed. "You tell Caesar?"

"Nah. But he thinks that if my mother and Julius weren't the ones to break the Pact, the Chinese would have."

"That's heavy. Aren't they supposed to be the most loyal motherfuckas?"

"I guess not," Boogie said and checked his phone for a missed call from Gino. There was nothing there. "Hey, when you go to the Island, I want you to do somethin'."

"Wassup?"

"I want you to take Morgan with you."

"Morgan? As in your sister?"

"Yeah," Boogie said and nodded. "Ain't really shit she can do with Harlem right now, and even when there is, Diana is gon' show her those ropes. But in the meantime, I want her to see how shit really goes in the field."

"A'ight, man." Bentley let out a breath. "I ain't never worked beside no girl though. So we'll see how it goes."

"Thanks, man. You're doing me a favor."

"I know, nigga. You ain't slick. This is shit you're s'posed to be doing." Bentley stood up and made like he was heading back toward the bedroom area of the house. "And your payment to me can be you lettin' me shower here and wear one of them fly-ass suits in your closet."

"Go right ahead," Boogie said with a laugh. His phone started to buzz in his pocket, and he answered it without looking. "This is probably Gino right now. Hello?"

"Ay, cuz, where the fuck are you at?" Tazz's frantic voice came through the other end of the phone.

"Tazz, what's wrong?" Boogie asked, sitting up straight.

The sudden change in tone of Boogie's voice made Bentley stop in his tracks and tune into the conversation. Boogie could hear a lot of commotion in Tazz's background, and he didn't understand what was going on.

"Man, cuz. It's Gino."

"What about Gino?" Boogie's brow furrowed.

"He's dead, man. He's fuckin' dead! They got him."

Chapter 15

Boogie had never seen Bentley look as distraught as he did while he stood in the morgue of the hospital in front of Gino's dead body. The two of them had waited until the detectives they saw lurking around had come and gone. Neither wanted to be questioned about anything going on around the city.

It was strange seeing Gino lying lifeless like that. Not just because they had seen him the night before, but because he had always been so full of life. Boogie couldn't believe that he was dead. He had always been so hard body. But there he was, gash in his neck with his soul missing. He was the last one that Boogie would have thought the game would take out, but it spared no one. They'd been told that Gino had been stabbed through the neck, and there was no way that he would've survived it.

"You a'ight, man?" Boogie asked just to fill the quiet air with some noise.

"Fuck no, I'm not. They killed my cousin. I should have never left him last night."

"Come on, man. You couldn't have known this was gonna happen."

"I should've known that it was a possibility. We at war. I should've never let him get involved with this man. He would still be alive."

"Nah, the person to blame, if anybody, is me. I feel like I keep taking these kinds of hits with salt. First, my dad was murdered by a man who was supposed to be his best friend. My mother turned on me and manipulated me to become someone I'm not. And now this. I'm sorry, bro."

"I'm not even gon' lie to you. I want to be mad. I want to be mad so bad, but the motherfuckas I need to aim my anger at ain't even in this room right now. But Gino knew what he signed up for. I'ma be sad for a minute he's gone, but he's gone. I'ma make sure his homegoing is real nice. In the meantime, we still have life. The question is, what are we gon' do with it? Business gotta continue."

"We gon' tighten up every loose screw. Especially since that shit happened at the Sugar Trap," Boogie said, clenching his fists. "Tazz said they rolled the cameras back in the club, but I didn't see shit. But that doesn't even matter though. We know that the Chinese are responsible for it. And you know what this means, right?"

"It means they don't give a fuck."

"Exactly. I need eyes and ears in the Bronx at all times. I need to know what the hell they're planning over there. And any motherfucker you see in Brooklyn, Harlem, or Staten Island who looks out of place? Kill 'em."

"Got it. Speaking of the Island, I'm about to get ready to head out. Let Morgan know I'm on my way to scoop her."

"Don't worry about that, G. I can send somebody else to handle it."

"Nah, I got it. Gino used to always tell me that one man don't stop the whole show. Business always has to continue."

"You sure?"

"I'm positive."

"Okay, I'll let her know you're about to come through."

Bentley slowed to a stop in front of Diana's home and honked twice to let Morgan know that he was outside. Boogie had already told her that Bentley was on the way to pick her up. He hoped that she didn't keep him waiting long, because he needed to stay on the move to keep from thinking about Gino. Eventually he would sit with it and accept it, but right then he wanted to think about anything else but Gino lying dead in a morgue.

He probably waited a total of three minutes before Morgan came bounding down the stairs. Her hair was pulled back and she wore a form-fitting pink Balmain pantsuit with a double-breasted blazer. She waved at him before she got in the car, and the first thing she did once the door shut was grab his hand.

"Boogie told me about Gino."

"I'm sure he did. Listen, don't—"

"No, you listen. I'm so sorry for your loss, Bentley. In the short time I was around y'all, I could tell that you and your cousin were close."

"We were." Bentley nodded. "He helped me and Boogie when he didn't have to. Look at where that got him. Dead."

"I hope you aren't blaming yourself."

"Tryin' not to. I keep tellin' myself that he knew the risks. But that still ain't sittin' right with me," Bentley said and then questioned himself about why he was being so open with her about his feelings. He shrugged his shoulders. "But business has to continue."

"It's okay to mourn. You know that, don't you?"

"I'll mourn once the Italians and Chinese learn their place."

Although Bentley could hear the sincerity in her tone when she spoke, he didn't have a better response for her. He pulled his hand away from hers and drove away from in front of the building toward Staten Island. Behind them, an SUV filled with their soldiers followed them. Boogie wanted to make sure that both Bentley and Morgan recovered. He didn't want what happened to

Gino to happen to them when they least expected it. After a few more moments of an awkward silence, Bentley cleared his throat.

"Did Boogie tell you why he wanted you to come with me?"

"Something about how he wants me to learn the game because I'll run Harlem one day. Blah, blah."

"Why 'blah, blah'?" Bentley asked, amused.

"Because how hard could it be? You lay down the law, make money, and sometimes you got to shoot a nigga. What's so hard about that?"

Bentley was surprised to hear himself laugh unexpectedly, mainly because, that easily, she'd summed up the life of a boss. Still, it wasn't as easy as she made it sound.

"Talking about the field and being in it are two completely different things."

"How different can they be?"

"Well, for starters, do you know how to lay down the law? Do you know how to talk to niggas, how to broker a deal, and how to ensure the motherfuckas under you are going to stay in line? You gotta make the streets respect you."

"From what I've seen working under Diana for as long as I have, you knew before I knew that she was my birth mother. People follow her because they fear her."

"Fear and respect go hand in hand, shorty, but they're two different things," Bentley schooled her as he drove. "A person can fear you and still snake you. Fear doesn't make a person loyal, and all Diana has around her are loyal people. That's from respect. Even in the war Boogie waged, Diana was the only one who was untouched. I can't even call her operation an empire. I'd have to say she's built a dynasty. A dynasty Diana picked you as the next person to lead. And do you know what I think?"

"What?"

"I think that she does so well because she has the essence of a woman but the mind of a man. She thinks and moves just like us. She learned how to fight and how to shoot just like us. If she was well enough and not injured, I guarantee you that she would be front line right now with the rest of us."

"Yeah, she's a tough cookie. I'll give her that."

"Well, it's time to turn you into the next tough cookie. Violence and death are everyday parts of this. Can you handle that?"

"I've been sleeping just fine so far," she said. "Now can you quit trying to test my temperature and tell me exactly what we're doing today?"

"Yeah, a'ight," Bentley chuckled. "Today we're going to Staten Island to, as you said, lay down the law. Ever since Boogie took over that area, the Italians have been movin' grimy. They killed some of our men, and we're sure that they are going to keep doing that until we offer them a deal."

"Why doesn't Boogie just off them then?"

"Because we're already into it with the Chinese. We don't have the time to fight a battle. Not when there is another solution."

"And the solution is?"

"We're going to offer them the opportunity to run their own territory under Boogie's rule, of course."

"Isn't that what he offered them at first? And didn't they turn him down?"

"It is. But that was before we were feuding with the Chinese. Now we both have a common enemy, because if they win the war, the Italians get nothing. Probably not even the lies. They might not want to accept Boogie as their new leader, whereas that's the smartest thing to do, because either way the coin is flipped, they never will have full control of Staten Island again. Because if he does decide to battle them, he'll wipe them out. So this offer is him being graceful."

"Well, let's just hope it goes well."

Chapter 16

The sound of Nicky's and Nathan's footsteps echoed on the white walls of the laundromat they walked through. Oceans of Suds was one of Caesar's many businesses in Manhattan. There were only a few people there washing clothes, and they knew not to pay the men wearing suits any mind. When Nicky and Nathan got to a thick door in the back, Nathan hit it one time with his fist.

"Open up."

"What's the code word?" a voice on the other end said.

"Nigga, it's me. Open this fuckin' door!"

There was hesitation, but after a couple of seconds, the sound of locks being turned could be heard on the other side. With a loud creak, the door swung open, and Nicky saw their cousin Ross on the other side. He was a big dude, bigger than both Nicky and Nathan put together. To his surprise, Nathan pulled out his pistol and put it to his neck.

"Nigga! Didn't I tell you never to open this door for anyone without the fuckin' code word?"

"It's you though! You crazy motherfucka!" Ross exclaimed with wide eyes.

"How did you know that? It coulda just been someone who sounds like me."

"There's a peephole on the door," Ross said and showed Nathan. "You put it there."

"Oh," Nathan said, looking at the peephole. He stepped away from Ross and put his gun away. "You still need to get the code word next time, nigga."

"Ay, Nicky. Ya brother is insane," Ross said.

"Tell me something I don't know," Nicky said, amused. "Now take us to see what we came for."

"Right this way, but keep that crazy-ass nigga by you."

Ross took them down a flight of stairs and down a hallway, where they encountered another door. He pulled out a ring of keys and unlocked it. On the other side of it were black women wearing scarves and masks working in what seemed to be a sweat shop. They were sewing clothes and packaging them, but Nicky knew that everything wasn't what it seemed. In between the fabric and jean pockets of the clothes they were stitching were Baggies of crack, cocaine, heroin, and ecstasy. When they were done, the clothes would be packaged and shipped to the correct boutiques that were also owned by Caesar. The drugs would then be separated and distributed. It was a system that had worked without issue for years. They walked past the women hard at work to a wall at the end of the room. Nicky looked around and put his hands up.

"Where is it?"

"You're lookin' at it," Nathan said and pointed at the wall.

Before Nicky could ask him to elaborate, Ross went to the end of it and pushed it to the side. The wall rolled like it was on wheels and revealed a large safe behind it.

"An illusion wall," Nicky said.

He stared at the safe in disbelief. They called the main stash "the vault." And he knew that he had told Nathan to switch the location of the stash spot, but he didn't know that he would go and build an actual vault. He gave a small laugh and shook his head at his brother as Ross opened the safe. When the last number of the code was input, there was a small click. Russ opened the safe door and revealed the contents inside. Nicky took in a breath of fresh air when he saw that everything looked to be there. From the top to the ground were stacks and stacks of money. There had to have been at least half a million dollars in that room. Caesar sent him to check on it to make sure it was all there since he'd been out of commission. Even though Nicky reassured him that it was, he understood the need to know.

"Good shit," he said and dapped Nathan up. "Now we need a total count. Ross, I'm gon' put you in charge of that. Have his girls finish up what they're doing and get to counting."

"You got it, G," Ross told him, running his dark hands together. "By the way, how is he doing?"

"Good. Just tryin'a make sure all his affairs are still in order."

"No doubt. Well, I'm fa sho' gon' be at the block party. I ain't ever in my life known anybody to come back from the dead before."

"I guess the truth was he was never dead."

"Yeah, you're right. Pshh. The streets are just crazy right now. You heard about that nigga Gino?"

"Gino? The cat who be rollin' with Boogie?" Nathan asked Ross.

"Yeah. They put that nigga on an icebox. They found him dead in the parking lot of the Sugar Trap. Word is he had one of them Chinese knives stuck in his neck. You know the ones that you see off that anime shit? I ain't even know that shit was real."

"Damn," Nicky said, because that was news to him. He turned to his brother with worry on his face. "Who all else knows about this spot?"

"Just the people in his room, and the niggas keepin' my watch outside."

"Okay. Well, I know I just had you move all this here, but I need to have you move at least half of it again.

There's too much product and money in this bitch, and if somehow the location of this spot were to leak, it will be too big of a loss. Can you make that happen for me?"

"Fa sho'," Nathan said and turned to Ross. "I want every bitch in this room to have a money counter. Make them bitches add that shit up, and let me know when it's done."

"It'll be done," Ross said.

Nicky dapped him up before he and Nathan made their exit. They left Oceans of Suds and went back to where Nicky's Mercedes was parked on the street. Once they were inside, Nicky told his brother they had one more place to stop.

"Nigga, I'm hungry," Nathan said as his stomach growled. "We can't stop and get a chicken on the way?"

"We can grab something to eat after. But Caesar wanted me to stop by Marco's place and do a well check. He was supposed to hear from him yesterday, but he never made contact."

"Well, hopefully that Mexican motherfucker whipped up some tacos or some shit 'cause I'm starving. Come on, *ándale, ándale*. Let's go!"

Chapter 17

There was never a day in Zo's life when he actively entertained the thought of living without his father. Of course he knew that one day Marco was going to die, but he always thought it would be of old age. Marco was always so cautious with his business moves and everything he did. He didn't go anywhere alone, not even to the grocery store. When Marco had told him that they were into it with the Chinese, Zo didn't take it as seriously as he should have. He thought that it would just be one of those things that blew over like every other beef his father had had with somebody. However, Zo learned just how serious it was that morning when they got an unexpected knock on the door.

Usually the help would answer the door, but that morning Zo thought he could be helpful since they were all busy making breakfast for the family. His father hadn't come home the night before, but that wasn't unheard of. There were many days when his father came strolling in the house at eight in the morning in clothes from the night before. And Zo was sure that that morning would be the same story. And because he was usually starving when he came home, Lorenzo's mother decided to have a feast made for him. She knew he had been stressed lately.

When Zo opened the front door, he was expecting to see somebody standing there, but there was nobody. Instead there was a rectangular box sitting on the porch. He didn't know why the dread set in right then, but it did.

Maybe it was the fact that he could see that the bottom of the box was wet. Slowly he walked to it and lifted up the top. It was a good thing that they did not have neighbors, because his bloodcurdling shout could be heard for miles. His mother, Christina, and his younger sister came running to see what had happened.

"What, *mijo?*" his mother asked with wide eyes. "Why do you scream like that? You upset the whole house."

Zo couldn't speak. His lips moved up and down, but no words came out. All he could do was point at the box on their porch with a shaky hand. Zo's sister, Daniella, approached the box first. Once she saw the contents, she doubled over and threw up everything in her stomach.

"Oh, my God," she cried while heaving. "Oh, my God, *Papi.*"

"*Papi?*" Christina asked, alarmed, and stepped forward to peer in the box. "Oh God. No! No! No!"

Zo caught her as she fell to the ground. Her body trembled so violently that it shook his body too. He buried her face in his neck so she could not see. Someone had made it their business to deliver Marco's severed head to them in such a sick way. Next to his head were Pedro's and Duan's, Marco's most trusted men. It was demented.

"Get her inside, Daniella. She doesn't need to see this," he instructed.

"Come on, *Mamá,* let's go in the house," Daniella said and took their mother from Zo. Before she went back in the house, she turned to her brother. "Find out who did it."

While she was gone, Lorenzo looked to the men who were supposed to be looking over the estate. They'd been watching the scene unfold curiously when Lorenzo waved them over to him. The only way anyone could have been let onto the property was through them.

"Who the fuck is responsible for letting someone through the gate without buzzing first? Huh?" he asked.

"It was me, sir," a Hispanic man by the name of Julio said. He had been working for Marco for the past few years, and Marco trusted him enough to watch over his home. He knew better than to do something so foolish.

Zo grabbed him by the side of the face and forcefully made him look into the box. When Julio saw what was inside, he gagged, but Lorenzo held his face still. The others looked inside and tried to hold in their retching, but some of them failed.

"I didn't know," Julio said.

"You would have if you had done your job right. Who came to the gate?"

"It was a deliveryman."

"And you didn't think about double-checking his credibility?"

"He was in a delivery truck. And he said he had a package for you, Lorenzo."

"And so you just let him through the gate?" Zo asked through clenched teeth and threw the man back roughly. "And you know we're into it with the damn Chinese! What did the motherfucker look like?"

Julio glanced at the other men fearfully before turning back to Zo. When he turned back to Zo, it was obvious that he didn't even want to speak. His bottom lip trembled when he finally opened his mouth.

"He . . . he was Asian, sir."

"What?"

"He was just a kid. I didn't think—"

"You're right. You didn't think!" Lorenzo screamed and saw red. He pointed at some of the men in front of him. "You four, after that delivery truck. The rest of you, take this sorry excuse of a motherfucker to the basement. I'll deal with him later."

"Zo, please. I have a family," Julio begged, but his cries fell on uncaring ears.

"Because of you, my *mamá* was allowed to see her husband in such a fashion. That will forever be unforgivable to me. You will be punished. Now get him out of my fucking sight.

"Yes, jefe," they said in unison.

They left him alone with the box of heads. Zo had too many emotions swarming around inside of him. Just as he was about to go inside of the house and find where Daniella had taken his mother, he heard the sound of a phone ringing. He looked around, but there was nobody out there but him. But the more he listened, he realized that the ringing was coming from inside of the box. Holding his breath, he knelt down, and sure enough, right next to his father's head, there was a flip phone. He knew that whoever was calling was calling for him. Reaching down, he took the phone out and flipped it open to answer it. It smelled terrible and had blood on it, and those were the reasons he didn't put it all the way to his ear, but he could still hear breathing on the other end.

"Hello?"

"Do you like my gift?" an amused voice asked. By the accent, Lorenzo could tell that the person was of Asian descent.

"Who is this?" he asked.

"My name is Tao Chen, nephew of Li Chen. I am now the new leader of the Chinese organization here in New York. And unfortunately, your father's time here has expired."

"Where is the rest of his body?"

"Somewhere on ice. I am familiar with your customs of burial and the Day of the Dead. So I want to give you the opportunity to give him a proper funeral. If you would like the rest of your father's body to be delivered to you, you have to do something for me."

"Go to hell."

"Oh, I will not make my arrival there for a while. But your father surely will."

"What do you want, Tao?"

"I want you to take the knee to me. Pledge your allegiance, and I will spare you and everyone in your camp."

"You want me to hand over Queens?"

"Precisely," Tao said like it was nothing, and Zo felt his blood boil.

"I think that if it's a choice between rotting in hell or handing over everything that he built to you, my *papá* would gladly rot for eternity."

"Your father lost his head when I asked him for much less. Are you sure you want to do this? You will just see more death in your family."

"Kiss my ass, you son of a bitch."

"So be it. Your entire family's blood will be on your hands. I will be seeing you, Lorenzo, son of Marco."

Click.

Lorenzo launched the phone at the concrete he stood on and watched it shatter into tiny pieces. Just as he was shouting his curses and war cries into the air, a silver Mercedes rolled in front of the house and parked in the circular driveway. Not expecting any company, Lorenzo did the first thing he could think of. He drew his gun and pointed at whoever was preparing to get out of the car.

"Whoa, whoa, whoa, man. Chill out. Caesar sent us. He wanted us to check on Marco."

Realizing that it was Caesar's nephews Nicky and Nathan in the car, Lorenzo stopped aiming the gun. Since Caesar and Marco had done such close business for years, Lorenzo had grown up with them. But right then he didn't have anything to say to them. He didn't know how to think, and he didn't know how to feel. The only thing that he could do was drop down on the steps, distraught.

"You good, Zo?" Nicky asked as he and Nathan approached cautiously.

Zo shook his head no. All of his feelings hit him hard at once, and he inhaled sharply as finally the tears started to fall. Not knowing Lorenzo to be an outwardly emotional man, concern registered on Nicky's face. He looked from Zo to the box he was sitting next to.

"What's that?" he asked.

"My *papá*'s head," Lorenzo choked out, and Nathan looked inside.

"There's three motherfuckin' heads in there!" he shouted at Nicky.

"Damn. That's Marco," Nicky said and let out the air in his cheeks. "Caesar is gonna blow a fuckin' gasket. Goddammit. Not Marco. How the fuck did it come to this? Do you know who did this?"

"Tao Chen," Zo answered. "He killed my *papá,* and now he wants Queens."

"Li's nephew," Nicky said. He placed a hand on Zo's shoulder and gave it a squeeze. "I'm sorry for your loss, Zo. But we're gonna make that slant-eyed bitch pay. Believe that."

Chapter 18

"Do you even know where to find the Italians?" Morgan's voice sounded after it felt like she and Bentley were just driving aimlessly around Staten Island.

The Italian mafia had been exiled from the borough by Boogie when he took over. However, some of them had been bold enough to stay. Since Boogie had been capitalizing on the separate drug operation on Staten Island, the Italians who stayed were giving him hell, killing his dope boys, burning the product, and harassing anybody they thought was in with Boogie. It wasn't enough to really stop business from continuing, but it was a thorn in Boogie's side.

"Of course I do," Bentley told her as he drove with one hand on the wheel.

His seat was low, and he was leaned back as he peered outside at the buildings they passed. It was almost as if he were a tourist who was sightseeing. They'd driven around the borough at least three times and hadn't stopped once. As they drove by, the people on the streets noticed them. They were everything but inconspicuous in the shiny black Mercedes with an armored vehicle following closely behind them. Some people turned their noses up, but most of the black people waved happily.

"Boogie changed a lot of their lives," Bentley told Morgan when he saw the confused look on her face. "When the Italians ran things over this way, they starved a lot of the lower-class citizens out. Mostly black."

"How?"

"Buyin' up all the businesses, not hirin' black. Shit like that. There was no opportunity for the ones livin' in poverty. So when Boogie took over, he changed that. He opened business and hired predominantly black. He opened that day care right there." Bentley pointed at a building they passed.

Morgan could tell that it had been newly constructed. It was completely fenced, and she watched as children played on the playgrounds. All smiles, no worries.

"Mothers can send their kids there at a low cost and know that their babies are safe while they go to work. And he opened that food pantry right there so low-income families will have dinner every night," Bentley told her and pointed at another building. "And he's in the middle of openin' a few early childhood learnin' centers here and in Brooklyn."

"Wow. I had no idea he was such a humanitarian," Morgan said and then glanced at Bentley. "Is that why you stood by his side when he was blowin' the city up?"

"Ay, chill out," Bentley laughed. "That's your brother you're talkin' about. Mine too."

"I'm just askin'."

"Boogie is a good dude. Usually a nigga would face his demise after some shit like that, but he's been given the chance to learn from those mistakes. And lucky for him, he got niggas like me who will war with the world to protect him while he's in class."

"You would die for him?" she asked.

"If it had to be that way, yeah."

"Why?"

"You don't meet too many motherfuckas like him in a lifetime. I believe in that nigga."

"You talk about him like he's a messiah or somethin'."

"You're seein' with your own eyes what he's doin' over here. Brooklyn has been untouchable since he took over, and he's even runnin' Harlem for Diana. Money hasn't declined once, even with the Chinese threat. Everybody's eatin' right now. Caesar can't even say he's done anything of that magnitude in so short of a time. He's gon' be great, and I'ma help see that through."

He grew silent after those words, and Morgan did too. She had spent time with Boogie, but she felt like there still was a rift between them. She could tell that he and Diana had some sort of bond that she wasn't a part of, but she was still trying to form a solid one with the both of them. It was nice to get to know Boogie through someone close to him. She could tell that Bentley wasn't saying those things just because he had to. She could feel that he meant them. Even the part about dying for him if he had to.

"Where are we goin'?" she asked.

"To that pizza shop on the corner right there. That's always been our end destination."

"We passed that already." She furrowed her brow at him.

"I know we did, but I wanted to cruise around and be seen so those motherfuckas know we're here. They'll be expectin' us now."

They pulled into the parking garage next to the gourmet pizza shop and parked. Before they got out, Bentley reached inside of the glove compartment. He pulled out a black Glock with a diamond-encrusted slide and handed it to her. She took it but made a face at it.

"A gift from Boogie," he said. "You do know how to use that, right?"

"I did used to work at the Sugar Trap, you know? I would never work in a place like that without knowing how to defend myself."

"I'm not askin' if you can defend yourself. I'm askin' if you know how to shoot a gun."

"I'm not scared to," Morgan said and rolled her neck.

"So much attitude. I was just askin', shorty. Shit, your brother stuck you with me. I just wanna know that if shit pops off, you gon' be straight."

"I'll be straight. And just for the record, anybody would be happy to be 'stuck' wit' my fine ass," she told him and pursed her lips.

"You are workin' it." Bentley jokingly cocked his head and licked his lips.

"Boy, let's go." Morgan turned her face so he wouldn't see her smile.

Bentley was fine. No, he was finer than fine. And Morgan knew he knew it. From his brown skin to his smile all the way down to his dope-boy swag that he could switch up at the drop of a hat. Like right then, rocking the Balmain double-breasted suit jacket with the matching slacks. She could tell that he was used to using his charm to get whatever he wanted, but Morgan wasn't that easy. But if he ever showed her that he was serious about making a move, she wouldn't tell him no.

They got out of the car at the same time as the goons behind them. The goons toted big guns and walked closely behind them. They entered the restaurant through a door inside the garage. As they walked by the dining hall on the top level, the delicious aroma of pizza being cooked flooded Morgan's nostrils. She loved pizza. It was one of her favorite dishes. If they weren't there on business, she would have sneaked away to grab a slice, but they walked right past it. Bentley seemed to know where he was going. They walked through the kitchen into the back of the restaurant where there was a door that was guarded by two Italian men wearing black suits. They were in the middle of laughing about something, but upon seeing

Bentley and Morgan approaching them, they grew serious.

"State your business," one of them demanded.

"I want to see Stefano."

"He's not expecting anyone. So I suggest you go back to where you came from."

"Is that what y'all said to Li'l Freddy and them before you killed them?"

"Little Freddy? Little Freddy?" The man tapped his chin like he was trying to remember something. "The short guy with the tall hair? Liked to wear bright colors?"

"That's him."

"Oh. I did him in myself." The man smiled and stepped slightly closer to Bentley. "You should have heard him screaming right before I sliced his throat, eh?"

He and the other man laughed loudly in Bentley's face. It was something they would live to regret. Bentley's fists struck like lightning. He punched the man who had done all of the talking in the throat and then followed through with a sickening blow to the face. Morgan heard his jaw break before he fell unconscious to the ground. When the second man reached for his gun on his waist, Bentley grabbed his arm and twisted so hard it came out of the socket. He went to shout in agony, but Bentley's fist had already connected with his mouth. He punched him again, and again, and again until his face was covered in blood and his eyes were no longer open. He fell down next to his partner and Bentley spit on their bodies.

"I liked Li'l Freddy," he growled and took the keys off one of their belt loops. "We'll let ourselves in this motherfucka."

The men behind them aimed their guns at the door as Bentley unlocked it. He pushed it ajar, revealing a lounge room on the other side. Half-naked white and Italian women walked around freely. Some were on the side snorting coke on the laps of men who fondled them. The other men stood around smoking and talking mess to each other. Bentley counted a total of eleven men to his five, including him. But the choppers in his boys' hands made him feel invincible. His eyes fell on one Italian man sitting in a chair at the back of the room behind a grand desk like King Tut. Every able body in the room noticed the newcomers at the same time and went for their guns.

"I wouldn't do that if I were you." Bentley wagged a finger. "See these niggas behind me? If they spot any of y'all pointin' a gun at me, they gon' let them things in their hands rip your bodies into shredded meat."

The Italians stared at the guns aimed at them and thought better about their next move. All it would take was one sweep to kill them all, and they knew it. Slowly their hands moved away from their waists.

"That's what I thought. Stefano! Just the man I was lookin' for."

"To what do I owe this unpleasurable intrusion?" Stefano, the man sitting at the desk, asked. "I just got news that you are moving about our streets."

"Yeah, and I was comin' in peace until your boys out in the hallway started talkin' that shit. I had to hurt 'em."

"Are they alive?"

"I think so, but I don't really care if they aren't," Bentley answered, and Stefano huffed out a small breath through his nostrils.

"What can I do for you, Bentley?"

"We came here lookin' for you." Bentley stepped forward and Morgan followed suit. Where he went she went.

Stefano looked to be about 40 years old, give or take a few years. He wasn't a looker at all with his grainy skin and thin chin. The hair on top of his head was oily, and his eyes were red. He was an average-sized man, and like every other Italian around him, he was dressed in a suit.

"'We'?" Stefano asked and let his eyes fall on Morgan.

"My colleague and I here have a proposition for you."

"I thought Boogie was your colleague. What are you doing here with this woman? You offend me," Stefano scoffed. "I didn't take Boogie for the foolish type to let a woman be the face of his operation."

"If I were you, I would tread lightly. You don't even know who is in your face right now."

"A woman I wouldn't mind fucking. You got some nice tits on you," Stefano said, and his men laughed.

"Watch your mouth. I would hate for Diana to learn that you're talkin' to her daughter in such a nasty way."

"Her what?" Stefano's eyes went wide at the mention of Diana's name. "Diana doesn't have any children. Not that I know of."

"Well, now you do," Morgan said, finally finding her voice. It came out stronger than she thought it would. But she couldn't stand a sexist, especially one who said such vile things. "And like Bentley just told you, we're here to talk business."

"And what business could you have with me?"

"Boogie exiled all of you when he took the throne, but yet you're still here on Staten Island doing business and collecting our money," Bentley told him. "Honestly, I should've come in here guns blazin'. Especially after what you did to my little niggas."

"We did that because you blacks came onto Staten Island and tried to take everything from us."

"We 'blacks' didn't try. We *did*," Bentley corrected him. "Your old boss, Bosco, is dead. And the reason why is because he plotted against the Tolliver family and made himself a threat to the other families. So your demise is your fault. This is Boogie's shit now, and you have one option. And that's to get with the fuckin' program."

"We did not leave when he so-called tried to exile us, nor did we stop making our own money in the streets of this borough. So why do you think we will listen now?"

It was the smug look on his face that did it for Morgan. Sitting there, acting all tough, Stefano really felt like he was untouchable. He really thought that he was the man, defying the laws of the streets and making his own as he went. Someone needed to humble him, and that someone was standing right in front of his face.

"Do you think that you're here because you're strong? Do you think that you're able to move around the city and make money because you're smarter than us?" Bentley asked as a slow and deadly smile spread across his face. "Because you would be wrong to think that. If we wanted to wipe all of you Italian scum out today, we could, and it wouldn't even take a whole day. The only reason you're still here is because you're so minuscule. You know that one toy a kid leaves out and you just happen to kick it and stub your toe? That's what you are. You're just a nuisance, not a threat."

Morgan watched Bentley's words register in Stefano's mind. It made her happy to see that same smug expression wash away just that quick. He sat up in his seat angrily and glared at the two of them.

"I don't like when people make idle threats."

"I can guarantee you there's nothin' idle about anything that I say. However, I understand that spillin' blood only leads to more spilled blood, and honestly, I'm tired of cleanin' that shit up. Which is why I'm tryin'a give you a choice."

"And I'm telling you I'd rather take my chances seeing how you hold up on the other end of that threat."

Stefano was still unmoved even after being humbled. It was typical narcissistic behavior. He was a man who couldn't or refused to understand that he'd been beaten.

"Why wait?" Morgan asked, and she did something that shocked everybody in the room.

She pulled the gun Bentley had given her from her waist and shot the nearest Italian to her. He shouted in agony and fell to the ground, clutching his leg where the bullet had entered.

"Anthony!" Stefano shouted. "You just shot my cousin!"

"And I'm going to kill him if you don't shut the fuck up and listen," Morgan said, aiming the gun at Anthony. She didn't know where the sudden wave of rage came from, but time was ticking, and Stefano was wasting every second of it. Her hand was still vibrating from the recoil of the first shot when she cocked the gun back again. "What Boogie's offerin' you is the chance to stay in your home. You would be able to make money in the sun and not in the shadows."

"Exactly," Bentley hopped in. "The difference between workin' for Boogie and workin' for Bosco is that now it's a larger money market for you. Before, you couldn't even do business in the other boroughs without starting war. Under Boogie you would be welcomed."

"And what if I don't want to work for anybody?

"Then we'll just kill you right here and let the new motherfucka in charge take our deal." Bentley's voice was flat and serious.

Stefano's eyes went from Bentley to Morgan and then to his cousin, who was whimpering in pain. As stubborn as he seemed to be, Morgan thought that he still was going to be defiant. But to their surprise, he nodded his head.

"Fine. We will agree to work for Boogie. As long as he agrees to supply us with product to sell, weapons, and an open market, we will agree to be of service to him."

"That's what I like to hear," Bentley said.

"Now you and this crazy bitch get out while I sulk in my defeat."

"I'ma let that slide just this one time." Morgan winked as she and Bentley turned to leave. "And it's not a defeat. It is the beginning of a beautiful relationship."

Chapter 19

Ming was a master of not showing any emotion on his face. But his body language spoke loudly. He wasn't too happy that his father was sending him on a mission with a black man, a man they only knew by the name Simon. He'd been given the chance to prove himself to Tao, and so Ming was given the responsibility of overseeing him and his actions. They sat quietly together in the front seat of a Rolls-Royce. Words hadn't been exchanged. Every once in a while, Ming glimpsed over at him. All he could think about was that the men who killed his uncle Shen were black.

"You don't like me very much, do you?" Simon finally broke the silence as he drove.

"What would make you think that?" Ming asked, unable to mask the sarcasm in his voice.

"You aren't doing a good job of hiding it," Simon told him with his eyes out the window.

Ming stared at him for a few moments and tried to read him. He was a calm man, confident. He didn't seem like the kind of person who let things get to him. But somehow he'd found himself entangled in a war that had nothing to do with him.

"I don't know you enough to dislike you. However, I don't like certain men who look like you."

"Look like me?" Simon asked, glancing at him. Ming pointed at the skin on his arm. "Oh, you mean black like me. I forget that you and the whites think we're all the same person."

"It might be a wrong observation."

"It *is* a wrong observation. Some might call it racist."

"I am no racist!" Ming snapped and then relaxed himself. "They killed my uncle. And when I'm done with them, I'll throw their bodies in the ocean just like I did Marco's."

"We share the same hate. But I don't blame you for feeling a way about me. Like you said, you don't know me, and I look like the men who you're at war with. But just know they're on my hit list too."

"That's what my father told me. What I don't understand is, what for? If I understand correctly, you are not even from New York. You have no reason to fight for the territories."

"And that's where you're wrong. Boogie Tolliver ripped my home apart by killing the kingpin, my brother. He killed my nephew, too. And like you I'm used to living a certain kind of lifestyle. I refuse to go back to fighting over scraps. So I'm going to help your father get what he wants. In return, Boogie dies and I get Brooklyn."

"How do we know we can trust you?" Ming asked curiously.

"You should never trust a man at face value. Trust is earned, not given, and I'm about to earn your trust right now," Simon said and pointed out the window. "The moment I left from meeting with your father, I started following Boogie. He moves around like there isn't a price on his head. He's a bold man, but that worked in my favor. It wasn't hard to spot him. It also wasn't hard to figure out who his hands were. Like him."

They'd been driving around the streets of Staten Island for what seemed like forever. At first, Ming thought that Simon had led them on a wild goose chase or was just wasting time. But then they slowed up on a gourmet pizza restaurant and watched as a Mercedes and a big black truck pulled into its parking garage. Not long after, the same two vehicles exited. The Mercedes drove past the Rolls-Royce, but the passengers paid them no mind.

"Almost every time I've seen Boogie, I've seen the man driving that Mercedes."

"What were they doing at an Italian restaurant?"

"When my brother Shamar was here, he was doing business with the then leader of this borough, somebody named Bosco. He was killed, so I can only guess the remaining Italians fell in line with Boogie. I think we should check it out."

"Lead the way."

Simon pulled the Rolls-Royce into the parking garage and got out to enter the restaurant. As they were walking in, there were Italian men rushing out, carrying another who seemed to have sustained an injury to his leg. Ming took a closer look and saw that he was bleeding profusely. He and Simon moved out of the way, and the men didn't give them a second thought. They exchanged a look before stepping inside. An Italian woman wearing her work uniform approached them as they neared the dining hall.

"I love your suits, boys!" Her voice was chipper, and her face was pleasant as she looked at the two of them. "A meal for two today?"

"No," Simon said, smoothing down his shirt underneath his jacket. "I'm here to see the man in charge."

"Oh, you would like to see the manager?" she asked, playing dumb.

"You and I both know what I mean by saying I want to see the man in charge. Take me to him now." Simon's voice was demanding as well as menacing.

"You . . . you must be talking about Stefano?"

"If that's the biggest man in charge, yes."

The woman looked from Simon to Ming, who glanced at her over his dark shades. After a few seconds, she nodded and motioned for them to follow her. She led them through the kitchen to a short hallway in the back of the restaurant. At the end of the hall was a door, and there were voices coming out of it.

"That damn Bentley!" an angry Italian voice was bellowing. "He thinks he can just come in here like that? And what good are you scumbags? Just letting him walk in here like that!"

When Simon and Ming walked through the door, they saw a room full of naked women, cocaine on tables, and armed Italian men. They all seemed to be taking a verbal beating from an angry man with a thin chin. Ming watched as he paced and continued to shout curses until Simon cleared his throat.

"Looks like you aren't having too good of a day," Simon said when all attention was on the two of them. "You must be Stefano."

"And who the hell are you?" Stefano cut his eyes at the newcomers. "I've had enough of uninvited guests for one day. Are you with Bentley?"

"If Bentley is the man I assume just left here, no, I'm not."

"I guess I should've figured that when I saw the chink with you." Stefano jerked his head toward Ming. "Who the fuck sent you? Tao from the Bronx?"

"I am Tao Chen's son, Ming Chen. What is your business with the man who just left here?"

"What's it to you?"

"Anyone who is in business with any other borough is an enemy of the Chinese," Ming told him.

"Well, then I guess we're enemies," Stefano said, throwing his hands up as if he didn't care.

"You have a choice. Join us, and help us claim Staten Island as a Chinese territory," Ming said and casually adjusted his diamond cuff links. "If not, you will die."

"You people and your choices today! You tell Tao to kiss my ass. I'll take my chances with the blacks. As much as I hate to admit it, they are winning, and they've been winning."

"Is that your final answer?"

"'Is that your final answer?'" Stefano mocked. "Get a load of this guy. At least Bentley had the smarts to come in here with shooters. It's just you and this bozo. Get the fuck out before I kill you and throw your bodies to my dogs."

Ming slowly looked around at the scowling Italian faces. Their guns were drawn but not aimed. They were trying to be intimidating, but Ming was not easily intimidated. His fingers brushed against his belt of knives under his suit jacket, and he gave a small nod.

"So be it," he said.

His hand moved so fast that it was a blur. Removing a kunai knife from his belt, he threw it at Stefano and pierced him through the forehead. Blood spilled from the wound, and Stefano was dead before he hit the ground. Every woman in the room screamed and ran out of the room. The men who were nearest to Stefano prepared to shoot, but Ming was too quick for them. He threw two knives at them, fatally catching them in the neck and the heart. Beside him, the sound of a gun firing repeatedly filled the room. It was Simon killing the rest of the men. When they were the only ones left standing over a bloody massacre of Italians, Simon tucked his still-smoking gun back in his pants.

"That went well," Simon said and then looked over at Ming. "Didn't anybody ever tell you not to bring a knife to a gunfight? Now on to the next target."

Chapter 20

"I heard you turned your gangster up."

Boogie's voice was followed with a small smile on his lips as he spoke to Morgan. He'd made the decision not to go to Marco's vigil since he had yet to be around Zo after everything he'd done. The two men were not close but knew of each other since their fathers did business. He just didn't know how Zo felt toward him and didn't want to make any already-open wounds deeper. Plus, Boogie knew firsthand how irrational a person could be after the loss of a parent. He would wait until Caesar spoke with him to set up a meeting. But Tao was hitting too close to home. First Gino, now Marco. So far he was up a body. So instead of being at the vigil, Boogie decided to stop by Diana's and talk to Morgan about how the meeting with the Italians went a few days before. He was sitting on the couch in Diana's living room while Morgan poured herself a glass of wine.

"Who told you that? Bentley?"

"You know that's who told me. You really shot that motherfucka?"

"I did," Morgan said. She looked at him with a shocked expression and then smiled. "I really did."

"How did it make you feel?"

"Powerful," she answered honestly and grew serious. "I don't like when anybody talks to me crazy. And Stefano was prepared to not respect me off the strength that I'm a woman. It made me so mad."

"Mad enough to make him feel you."

"And I did. It was gonna be my way or my way."

"I'm proud of you. I hope you know that."

"Yeah, yeah," Morgan said and took a sip of her wine.

"You may just have potential yet, young one."

"Do I need to remind you that we're pretty much the same age?" she asked and turned her nose up.

"I guess you're right," Boogie said, spreading his arms out on the couch. "Do you know how cool it would have been to have a sister growin' up?"

"I know what you mean," Morgan said, coming to sit next to him on the couch. "I always wanted a brother. You know, to protect me from bullies and stuff like that."

"You used to get bullied?"

"Hell nah. People weren't crazy, and I had a temper as a kid. I'm just saying it would've been nice to have a brother just in case that did happen."

"Well, you got me now, and I ain't gon' let nobody touch you . . . ever," Boogie said absentmindedly with his eyes on his jeans and Timberlands. When he looked up at her again, he caught her staring at him fondly, and he pretended to be grossed out. "Don't do that. I don't do well with that mushy shit."

"Whatever. It's just . . ."

"Just what?"

"I grew up having a family, but I never felt like I belonged. I just always felt different from everybody else. They didn't understand me, and now I've only known about you guys for a short period of time, and I've never felt more at home."

"You just finally found your tribe, that's all. You were born a princess. Destiny just finally brought you back to your throne. And from what Bentley told me, you're a natural at all of this shit. I don't think Diana is going to have anything to worry about."

"You think so? I don't think I'll ever be able to do what she does. Or be as good as her at it."

"I used to feel the same way about myself when it came to my old man. I didn't want none of this shit. Not the crown, not the work, nothing! I was in college to be a chef."

"A chef?" Morgan asked, laughing. "You can cook, like for real? No cap?"

"Hell yeah, I can cook, girl! I throw down, too! I haven't done much of it lately, but yeah. Cooking used to be my passion. That's all I could see myself doing at one point in time. I didn't want to become who my father was."

"What changed?"

"I realized that he never wanted me to be who he was. He just wanted me to be better than him, no matter what it was I chose to do."

"Then why did you choose to take over for him?"

"I'm just good at this shit. I'm a better boss and a better hustler than any kind of chef I would have become. One day I had to look in the mirror and accept it. No matter how fast and hard you try to run away from your destiny, the universe will always put you back on that path."

"So I learned two things about you today. Apparently you can cook, and your ass thinks you're Confucius."

"Get out of here!" Boogie found himself laughing hard.

"I'm serious. You are something new every day, B," Morgan said, laughing too. "For real, you really are good at this shit. I see the way the men around you look at you. They look up to you. So if there's anything that I can say to you, it will be to stop being so hard on yourself about what you did. Every great man makes mistakes, but an extraordinary man owns up to them."

"Thanks, sis," he said, and she gave him a funny smile again. "What now?"

"That's the first time you ever called me sis."

"That's what you are. Bonded by blood."

"You're right, I am. And I never got a chance to thank you for saving my life. You killed your own mother behind me. I—"

"We don't even have to talk about that," he said, cutting her off. "But of everything I did, the thing I made amends with first was killing my mother. She never loved me. She couldn't have. And if I hadn't killed her first, she would've killed me, or plotted to kill me like she did my dad. So you don't have to thank me for that. I did it for the both of us."

Before they knew it, the two of them were embracing. The things that had been left unsaid aloud were said in spirit. When Morgan pulled away, she had tears in her eyes.

"I thought I said I don't like the mushy shit," he said and got up. "When Diana gets back, tell her that I stopped by."

"You're about to leave? I thought you might like to show me these cooking skills that you have."

"Maybe next time. I need to get home to Roz and the baby."

"Give them my love. Hopefully I'll get to meet them soon after all this dies down."

"You already know. I'm going to keep my family tight this time. I'll stop by tomorrow."

Boogie gave her one last hug when she walked him to the door, and he left. As always, he had parked his car in front of Diana's building not too far away from the alley next to it. As he walked, he took notice of something strange—nothing. There was no movement on the block at all. Usually when he left that late at night, Diana's goons would flash their lights at him. But that night, the black Audi SUV sat idle. Boogie squinted and couldn't even see any movement inside of it. He felt the hair on the back of his neck stand up. Something was wrong.

He headed toward the SUV to see what was up. He wasn't even halfway there when he heard footsteps rushing toward him from the alley. He didn't have time to react. Before he could turn around, he felt steel on his temple and a strong arm around his neck.

"Make a sound and I'm gon' blow your head off, little nigga."

The voice that spoke was one he didn't know, but he recognized the malice in his tone. He was out for blood.

Chapter 21

"So you're this Tolliver nigga everybody keeps going on and on about?" Boogie's captor pressed the gun harder against his temple when he spoke.

Boogie's arms were free, but he didn't want to risk making any sudden moves. He couldn't see if the man's finger was on the trigger. So instead he stayed as still as he could.

"Yo, who the fuck are you?" Boogie growled.

"As far as you're concerned, I'm the Grim Reaper."

"Well, how the fuck do you know me?"

"You made it my business to know you."

"Well, if you're about to kill me, I suggest you do it quick before the Dominicans watchin' this block leave you leakin' on the concrete."

"Cute. You think them niggas are still alive," the man said with a laugh. "I guess I should have started with telling you don't be looking for anybody to come save you. I killed everybody watching the block. You know it's easy to sneak up on a man when he's busy watching one home. And you should really switch up your routine. Of everything you do during the day, this is the one thing you do every day. It wasn't hard for me to find you tonight."

"It's nice of you to let me know that you've been stalking me, but I would really like to know who my secret admirer is."

"Well, well, well, what do we have here? A killer and a comedian in one. I wonder if Shamar and Shane thought you were so funny before you killed them."

"Shamar and Shane?" The mention of those names sparked Boogie's curiosity even more. "Who are you?"

"You didn't think that you would be able to kill my nephew and my brother and just get away with it, did you?"

"You're Shamar's brother?"

"His baby brother to be exact. Simon's the name. And what you did caused mayhem back at home. Hell, I can't even call it that anymore. I don't have a place there."

"You can't blame anybody but yourself for being home-less."

"I didn't mean literally, stupid motherfucka," Simon said, squeezing his arm around Boogie's neck tighter. "I mean, everything is chaotic. Everybody's trying to be king. The chessboard is all fucked up. Shane was the one who kept the order. And with him gone, everything went up in smoke. People going to prison left and right, everybody's robbing everybody. I don't want no part in that."

"So you come here to play a part in what exactly?"

"For starters, I want your head on a fucking stick for what you did."

"I figured that's why I have a gun to my head. I'm not askin' you to state the obvious."

"You're really a funny one. Smart-mouth-ass nigga," Simon chuckled. "The other thing I want is a piece of the pie. A piece of that Chinese pie."

"I should've known they would be written all over this. Your family hasn't done anything but irritate the fuck out of me. You know that?"

"Well, with what the Chinese have planned for y'all, you won't have to worry about being irritated much longer."

"And what are they plannin' if you know?"

"I know a little somethin' somethin'. But you don't have to worry your pretty little head with that. The only things you need to be worried about are your last words."

"How about fuck you, motherfucka!"

Morgan's voice came from out of nowhere. She ran up behind Simon and hit him in the back of the head with a crowbar, forcing him to fall to the side and drop the gun. Boogie had never been happier to see her in his life. But he wasn't able to show his gratitude right then and there. Simon was trying to reach for the gun. Boogie kicked it out of his reach and drew his own pistol. He cocked it back and prepared to open Simon's face up, but something told him not to. Before Simon could make another move, Boogie hit him in the temple with the butt of his gun, knocking him out cold.

Marco's vigil was a sad event that was held in the backyard of his home. Only the closest members of his family were allowed to attend, and they all had long faces as they said their goodbyes. All day they ate and drank together while swapping stories about their experiences with Marco over the years. Later in the night, Caesar and Diana sat to the side and watched as his family lit candles for him under the night sky. They circled his casket and said prayers.

"I don't know if I'm sadder that he's gone or that there's only a head in the casket."

"I think it's both for me," said Caesar. "What a horrible way to die. He deserved better."

"He did."

When Caesar didn't hear from Marco after he went to meet with the Chinese, he thought the worst. But it didn't stop him from hoping for the best. However, that hope was killed when he got the phone call from Nicky saying what was delivered to his doorstep. Although Marco wanted to go to the meeting, Caesar knew he had the power to stop it, and he didn't. His thirst to have a man on the inside had been greater than Marco's well-being at the time. He would regret that for the rest of his life. Now the only men in the world he considered both colleagues and brothers were dead.

"That could've been us, you know." Diana's voice was somber as she stared at the white casket.

"It was almost us. But we're still here for a reason."

"And what reason is that? To watch each other die?"

"No. To grow our next generation."

"Who's going to groom Marco's son? At least Boogie had you."

"And Lorenzo will have Boogie. We have to keep them close. Our generation failed. We were able to keep the peace in the streets for a while, but our houses fell apart from the inside out. That won't happen with them."

"How do you know that?"

"Because instead of the Five Families, they will just be one. All of them together. That's where we went wrong. No matter how we tried to pretend to be a union, we were always just five families. There was always underlying animosity, and I might've been the one who added fuel to the fire. Always walking around like the only king of New York."

"Barry was always the one to humble you though."

"And now he's not here." Caesar felt a rush of sadness as he thought of Boogie's father. "You two should have tried to make it work. It might've been a good thing."

"We should have. But it would've cost too much turmoil. Too much pain."

"Well, as you can see, the pain part was inevitable." Caesar nodded toward the casket. "I don't even want to think about what Tao did to his body."

"How does something like this happen? Marco was one of the most cautious men I knew. I'm hearing people saying it was his old age that caught him slipping, but

I don't believe that. Not for a second. There's no way Tao was just able to kill him like that. There has to be something deeper."

"Diana," Caesar said, inhaling deeply.

"I know that look. You know something, don't you?" Diana asked, studying Caesar's face for the answer.

"The night before Marco's head was delivered to his doorstep, he met with the Chinese."

"What?"

"When Li was alive, he made an agreement with Marco, a kind of alliance. Marco would keep an eye on me for him, and in return, if anything whatever happened to the Pact, the two of them would side together against the rest of us."

"He was double-crossing you?"

"Never. Marco was one of the most loyal men I've ever met. He told me about the alliance right after it happened to warn me about Li. I allowed it to continue and used it to my advantage. The truth is I never trusted Li. Not after his father went to war with me. And not knowing what I know about their family."

"What about their family?"

"They're part of the Triad."

"The Triad?" Diana breathed. "You never told me."

"I never in my lifetime thought that there would be a time when I had to. The way I wouldn't want anyone to feel threatened by my power in Manhattan, I tried to give the same respect in the Bronx. Marco was the only other person who knew. And that's why he went the other night to find out what they're planning."

"So you knew he was going to meet with Tao? And you didn't stop him?"

"I did. He wanted to help."

"That was a suicide mission, Caesar, and you knew it."

"I knew the danger," Caesar agreed. "And I will forever live with the consequences of that. I never wanted Marco to die."

"Well, he did. And now we have yet another young boy at the head of his family who is not ready for the responsibility."

Diana had never looked at Caesar the way that she was looking at him right that second. It was a look of shock, disbelief, and disgust. She opened and closed her mouth a few times to say something but seemed to think better of it. She stood up and left him sitting there by himself. When she left, Nicky came and took her place.

"Unc, this might not be the best time, but a few community leaders approached me the other day."

"About what?"

"They want to throw a block party in Manhattan in your honor. To celebrate your life."

"You're right, now isn't the best time," Caesar said, looking at Diana, who had gone to sit by Christina.

"If that's the case, there will never be a good time. I think it will be a good look. Just to show the city that you're still here and on top of shit. They're expecting an answer soon. Plus, they already made the flyers."

"Fine," Caesar told him, still looking at Diana, who was avoiding his eye contact. "Fine, tell them yes."

"Good," Nicky said, looking from Caesar to Diana, who was blatantly ignoring him. "What's that about?"

"Nothing. Diana is just overrun with emotions about Marco's death. We all are."

"Yeah. Zo ain't doing too good over there himself." Nicky pointed to Lorenzo, who was sitting by himself drinking a beer.

"He'll learn to walk his own path without his father. Just like you did."

"I had you to help me with that."

"And he will have you and Boogie to help him."

"I don't know how I'll do that. Hell, I barely know what I'm doing most days."

"That's because you're a natural at it. You don't think. You just do." Caesar patted him on the leg.

"Speaking of doing, what are we gon' do about this Chinese problem? I feel like we're sitting ducks and just waiting for them to hit us. They've gotten their lick back twice, so now what?"

"It's time we make an offer."

"And if they don't accept? Which we know they won't."

"Then we hit them. But in the meantime, we need to find out as much information about the operation as possible. Because the first hit on them will be the last."

Nicky's phone began to vibrate in his pocket. He almost didn't answer it, but he thought it could be important. When he looked at the screen and saw who it was, he answered before it could vibrate again.

"Yo, Boogie, is everything good on your side of the trenches?" Nicky asked and paused. "What? A'ight. I'm on my way."

"What happened?" Caesar looked curiously at his nephew when he hung up the phone.

"Somebody just tried to make a hit on Boogie, and he caught the nigga. I'm about to get over there real quick."

"Take Lorenzo with you. He needs a change of scenery."

"No doubt. I'ma get up with you, Unc."

Caesar watched as Nicky went up to Lorenzo and said something in his ear. Lorenzo nodded and left with him after giving his mother a kiss on the cheek. There was a time when Caesar would have been the one to head out and see what was going on. But the truth was that his body was still tired. He wouldn't be any help in the field in his current state. For the first time ever, he was leaving the action to somebody else.

Chapter 22

Slap!

"Wakey wakey, dumb nigga!" Nathan backhanded Simon so hard that he rocked the chair Simon was bound to.

"Damn, bro! We need the motherfucka conscious, not dead!" Nicky pulled his brother back and gave him a wide-eyed look.

"My bad. I don't know my own strength at times," Nathan said and shrugged.

Nicky gave Boogie an apologetic look as Simon came to. Boogie had called Nicky to meet him in Harlem, and he brought Lorenzo and Nathan with him. They were going to take Simon in the alley next to Diana's and deal with him there. However, they didn't want to risk the chance of being seen. Lorenzo had the idea of moving Simon to one of Marco's garage warehouses to interrogate him.

"Mmm," Simon groaned, regaining consciousness. He opened his eyes and squinted at the bright overhead light. He tried to move his arms, and when he realized he couldn't, that was the moment he noticed he wasn't alone. Slowly he looked around at all of the weapons on the walls and tables around them. "Where am I?"

"For you? Hell," Boogie spoke, standing in front of him.

"Why didn't you just kill me? You had the perfect opportunity to."

"Because I think you have some information for me."

"I don't have shit for you."

"Then maybe I should just kill you now." Boogie pointed his gun at the middle of Simon's forehead.

"Go ahead. Killing me isn't going to stop what the Triad has planned for you."

"The Triad?" Boogie said and furrowed his brow.

"Oops, I've said too much," Simon said sarcastically.

"Nigga, that shit ain't real," Nathan said. "This ain't no movie."

"Oh, I assure you it's very real, and they're here in New York as we speak. Soon those precious empires you've worked so hard to build will be theirs. And you'll just be a memory."

"What do they have up their sleeve?" Boogie asked.

"Now why the fuck would I tell you that?" Simon looked at Boogie like he was stupid.

"What business do you have with them?"

"I was just supposed to kill you and get you out of the way. You should be proud of yourself, young man. You've made *quite* the name for yourself. The Chinese consider you their biggest threat."

"Well, now they should consider *me* their biggest threat," Zo's voice sounded as he glared at Simon.

"And you are?"

"Lorenzo Alvarez."

"Oh, you're the boy of the motherfucka who got his head chopped off," Simon taunted him, and Zo wasn't able to hold back. He stepped forward and punched Simon repeatedly in the face until his nose leaked blood.

"Chill." Boogie finally stepped in before Zo could hit him again.

"They threw the rest of his body in the ocean with the fishes. How did it feel to only have a head to bury?" Simon kept going.

It took both Boogie and Nicky to hold Zo back, even though Boogie really wanted to let him go. The things

Simon was saying about Marco weren't right, and he could feel his own blood boiling. He put his hand on Zo's chest to tell him that he had it. When Boogie turned back to Simon, he delivered his own powerful blow to his face. Simon grunted from the pain of the punch, and blood from his mouth splattered to the floor. Still, that didn't stop him from talking.

"It's ironic, isn't it? That all of you standing here before me are angry about things that you do to other people's families too."

"The Chinese are pissin' off more people than I ever did right now," Boogie retorted. "Why are they so confident?"

"*Now* you're asking the questions that need to be asked. Have you ever played chess, Boogie?"

"I haven't played in a while. But I know the rules."

"Then you're familiar with the objective of the game. The goal is to defeat the king, right? And right now Tao sees that as you. You have the most controlling power in New York right now. And what's the best way to kill the king?"

"You tell me."

"Destroy all of his allies. Even the pawns. Like say, Stefano."

"You killed Stefano?" Boogie asked.

"Like I said earlier, it's easy to sneak up on a man when he's only paying attention to one thing. You and your people are only looking for motherfuckas with slanted eyes. Not people who look like you. It wasn't hard to follow you and figure out who the closest people are to you. It also wasn't hard to follow them while they made their moves. I found my way to Stefano shortly after they left him. His and his boys' bodies are probably still down there stinking after what we did to him."

"Well, I guess it's a good thing that Stefano didn't have a big part in the grand scheme of things." Boogie kept a poker face although he felt a twinge of annoyance.

Stefano being knocked off the board didn't change much. Ultimately, however, Boogie was counting on the Italians siding with them. There was strength in numbers.

"It doesn't matter. Because soon everything you love and care about is going to be in the dirt. For example, your girlfriend and her daughter? They have an expiration date."

At the mention of Roz and Amber, Boogie put cement in his face again. That time his head bobbed like a bobblehead. He had shown where his true weakness was, but he didn't care. Threatening their safety was a surefire way to die.

"You're doing a lot of talking for someone who is tied to a chair," Nicky commented, stepping forward.

"That's because I can back it up."

"And how are you so sure? You're about to die."

"I don't think so." The confident way that he spoke made Boogie and Nicky look at each other.

Suddenly Simon began to laugh uncontrollably. His face was so badly beaten that smiling had to be very painful. But still, he laughed away.

"Yo, what the fuck is so funny, B?"

"All of you standing here. Boogie, the one thing that you need to know about me is that I never go anywhere without a plan B and C. I had complete confidence that I would kill you, but unfortunately I was wrong. But I had a failsafe put in place."

"Oh, yeah? And what was that?"

"Lift up my shirt and see."

Boogie gestured for Zoe to go lift up Simon's shirt. When he did, they saw a small device taped to his chest. Taking a closer look, Boogie noticed that there was a small white light flashing on it.

"What is that?" Nathan asked.

"Just in case I wasn't able to kill you, I took a chance that you might not kill me either. Now that probability was really low, so all of this is your fault, really. You should've killed me in Harlem. Because now the Chinese have been checking our location this entire time."

Boogie's eyes enlarged. He aimed his gun back at Simon's head and placed his finger on the trigger. Right before he was able to squeeze, the loud sound of glass shattering filled the garage warehouse. A smoke bomb had been thrown inside, and their surroundings began to get cloudy. Boogie tucked his face inside of his shirt to keep from choking. Soon after, the bullets started to rip. He had no choice but to leave Simon alive and jump for cover. Red beams invaded the garage trying to find a target, and more bullets followed.

"The back!" Zo shouted in the near distance. "Follow me!"

Boogie peered around the shelf he was hiding behind and saw Nicky and Nathan crouched following Zo. He glanced back at Simon, who was still tied to the chair. Simon saw him and winked.

"You can't run forever, boy."

Soon after, the garage began to flood with people shouting in Mandarin. Boogie didn't waste any more seconds. He ran after the others. Zo took them to a secret shaft door in the floor and yanked it open. It led to an unfinished basement. When they were all down there safe and sound, Zo pulled the hatch back down and ran down the stairs.

"This way." He waved for them to follow him. "This is a tunnel that leads to another building nearby. My *papá* had it built years ago just in case the Feds ever tried to come down on him."

They moved with a purpose and got to the other building in minutes. That building turned out to be a garage too, but instead of weapons, there were cars. Marco had been a very smart man. They all piled in a Dodge Caravan and drove away from the scene.

"Fuck. I wish I'd gotten the chance to bust on one of them chink motherfuckas!" Nathan growled from the back and hit his seat.

"Me too." Zo nodded as he drove. "But the way to avenge my *papá* isn't to go on a suicide mission. There were too many of them. We would have died or been taken prisoner."

"Yo, Boogie, you knew that nigga?" Nicky asked, glancing out the window to make sure they weren't being followed.

"I had a few run-ins with his family," Boogie answered. "But Simon? That was only my second time meeting him."

"From the sounds of it, it won't be the last either."

Chapter 23

"I want triple the men and round-the-clock security on my home. How could one man come and do this much damage?"

Diana's voice was loud and angry as she addressed everyone in the conference room. She had called an emergency meeting at the Sugar Trap after she found out what happened in Harlem while she was at Marco's vigil. Not only had someone penetrated her security, but two of her cousins were dead. To make matters worse, Morgan had been home. Granted, she saved Boogie's life, but Diana didn't know what she would have done if something had happened to either one of them. She thought she had done a great job at tightening up security around her home, but apparently it was not good enough. It was blowing her mind that one man came in and took out all of hers. Even more so when she found out who the man, Simon, was. The brother of Shamar Hafford. The same one who had conspired to kill Caesar.

"It seems like we just can't get away from these Hafford pests. And this one is working with Tao. I hope he's the last of them, because when I'm done with him, I don't want to see anybody connected to their bloodline." She stopped her rant and turned to one of her younger cousins. "Alex?"

"Yes, Diana?"

"How is your mother holding up after she heard the news about Armond?"

"She's not doing too well. She hasn't come out of her room since she heard the news."

"Send her my love, and let her know I will cover all funeral costs and anything else she needs."

"I'll let her know."

Diana felt horrible about what happened to Alex's older brother. Although Armond knew what he signed up for, he was still her blood. Who would have thought he'd be killed in a place that was supposed to be untouchable? But then again, they were at war, so nowhere was untouchable. She didn't plan on letting his death be in vain, and regardless of whether Caesar was ready to make his move on Tao, Diana was about to make hers. First Gino was killed in the Sugar Trap parking lot, then Marco, and now this. It was time to let the Chinese know who they were dealing with.

"Do what I told you. I don't want anybody with slanted eyes anywhere near Harlem or the Sugar Trap. I don't care who they are. Kill them on sight."

"Yes, ma'am."

As her cousins filed out of the room, she noticed one person had stayed behind. Morgan had been sitting off to the side during the meeting, but when it was over, she came and sat by Diana.

"You okay?" Morgan asked.

"I should be the one asking *you* that."

"I'm good. Me and Boogie did what we had to do."

"I really don't want to say it, because I'm so glad that you know who you are now, but I hate that I brought you into this lifestyle. You're not built for it."

"Excuse me? I just saved Boogie's life by knocking a motherfucka out. Not to mention I'm the one who got the Italians in line."

"You mean the same Italians who were found dead?"

"Dead?" Morgan was genuinely shocked.

"Yes, dead. Courtesy of Simon Hafford. The man who, for some reason, you and Boogie let live."

"Boogie wanted to question him."

"And look how well that went," Diana said dryly.

"That wasn't Boogie's fault. How are you supposed to know that—"

"In order to be a leader, you have to expect the unexpected! Ugh. Maybe we were wrong in thinking that you guys would be able to take over. You aren't ready."

"Well, maybe if you didn't keep me holed up in your house, I could get ready. Boogie seems to be the only one who wants to show me the ropes." Morgan's voice came out angry.

Diana had to catch herself and remember that she wasn't talking to Morgan her employee anymore. She was talking to her daughter. And looking at Morgan's face, Diana could see that her words had hurt her. She exhaled and rubbed her eyes with two of her fingers.

"I'm sorry, Morgan. About everything. I've never had to be a mother before. And now that I do, I just worry about your safety. Because if anything happens to you, it will be my fault."

"Well, if anything happens to me, I want to be able to defend myself. Like how you can. Remember when you dropped Tazz? You did that like it was nothing, and you're, uh, well, you aren't young anymore."

"Watch yourself."

"I'm just sayin'! I want to be able to do that. And I'm not gonna learn that sittin' in your kitchen drinkin' wine and watchin' Lifetime all day."

"You're right. And you'll learn how to fight soon, but—"

"But I'm not ready," Morgan groaned.

"Actually, I was going to say that first you need to learn how to shoot. There isn't enough time to teach you how to fight right now, but if you're ever in trouble, you are going to need to know how to shoot your way out."

"I already know how to shoot."

"Oh, yes, I heard you shot an Italian. Tell me, where did you mean to shoot him?"

"Where I hit him. His leg," Morgan answered but looked away.

"I'll ask again. Where did you mean to shoot him?"

"His stomach," Morgan finally answered truthfully under her breath.

"And that's exactly why you need to know how to shoot. When you really know how to work a gun, you understand that it's just an extension of yourself. Before you even pull the trigger, you'll know exactly where you're sending your bullets. Whether it's a still or moving target, a lethal or a nonlethal shot, you'll hit your mark every time. And I'm going to teach you."

"When?"

"Now. Let's go."

She had thoughts of taking Morgan to the gun range for the rest of the day. Morgan jumped up quickly, and the excitement read on her face. Maybe she was built for that life. Anybody else would have run for the hills, but she welcomed the game. Not only that, but she wanted to learn it. She and Diana had just left the conference room when Alex came running down the hall back toward them.

"Diana!"

"What? What's wrong?" she asked, recognizing the look of unease on his face.

"You have to come and see," he said. "In your office."

Something told her that, whatever it was, Morgan didn't need to see. Diana turned to her and grabbed her hands. She stared into her daughter's curious eyes and forced a smile to her face.

"Go wait in the car for me. I'll try to make this quick."

Morgan's eyes went from her mother to Alex. It was obvious she knew something was going on. Diana was just happy that she didn't press the fact. Morgan nodded her head, took Diana's keys, and walked away. Once Diana couldn't see her anymore, she turned back to Alex.

"Okay, now what is going on?"

"Come on," he said.

The two of them walked through the Sugar Trap to her office. Her girls were doing their jobs and entertaining the paying customers, and she could see that all of the private rooms were filled. But she didn't care about any of that. She wanted to know what was so important that he had to show her right then. A putrid smell hit her right before she stepped into her office.

"What the hell is that? It smells like something died!" she asked, plugging her nose.

"Not what, who. And it smells like that because someone did die," Alex said and pointed to the far wall at an open rectangular crate. "She was delivered today. We weren't going to open it. We thought it was something important for you, but then the smell started to set in."

"She?" Diana asked and walked toward the crate.

When she looked inside, she almost threw up. There, in fact, was a body inside. But not just any body. It was one of her girls. Her stage name was Desire, but her real name was Dezeray. She had been young, only 21. Diana could see she had been killed by a stab wound to the heart. She stared at the body for what seemed like forever. She looked so bad. She had to have been dead for days.

"How did this happen?" Diana whispered.

Alex didn't answer. That prompted her to turn around and face him. What she was met with was a guilty expression.

"We didn't want to worry you while you were taking your leave," he said and swallowed a lump in his throat.

"Worry me with what exactly?"

"One of the Chinese men—Shen, Tao's brother—reached out to us and said he had some information about what really happened with Li's murder. But what he was saying was real vague. It . . . it was agreed that Desire would go and get the information and—"

"Who made this call?" she asked, and he hesitated. "If I have to rip the information out of your throat, I will."

"Boogie," Alex told her. "Boogie called the shots."

"Boogie let one of my girls go with the Chinese? Is he out of his fucking mind?"

"I believe he truly thought he was going to get some information. She was supposed to bring it back, but she never did."

"And what did he think when she never returned?"

"The worst," Alex admitted. "And that's why we didn't want to tell you yet. Not in your weakened state."

"That idiot. He sent her into a setup."

"He didn't think so, Diana. He thought Shen was sincere. I think he was too."

"How could he have been when Desire is dead?"

"Because he's dead too. They killed him. They're blaming the blacks. So Caesar's camp or Boogie's. It's been real hush-hush for the moment. We just found out today. But it's getting around."

Diana's forehead wrinkled at his words. If Tao's brother had been killed, why had nobody heard about it? *Unless . . . unless it was an inside job.* But what would be so bad that Tao would have his own brother killed? It was too much to think about and was making her head hurt. She motioned a hand toward the crate.

"Get her out of here, and have someone clean my office. I want this smell gone. Matter of fact, have someone scrub down the whole building. Make sure you send Desire's family a check, and cover funeral costs. I need to talk to Boogie."

Chapter 24

"You idiot!"

Days had passed since what happened in the warehouse, but Daniella was just finding out about it. And when she did, she looked all around their family property to find Zo. She finally located her brother in their father's shed as he was sitting there piecing together guns that Marco never finished. He groaned when he heard her snatch the door open and barge inside. He could tell by the way her long ponytail whipped left and right when she rolled her neck that she was pissed off.

"*Stupido!*" she shouted, waving her arms in the air. "How could you be so stupid?"

"Now just isn't the time, Ella," Zo said as he prepared to put the slide on the Glock in his hands.

Not one to like being ignored or dismissed, Daniella went and snatched the parts from his hands. She slammed them on the table and shoved his shoulder.

"It wasn't the time the other night either. When you left *Papá*'s vigil to go do the *stupid* shit that you did. What were you thinking, eh?"

"Boogie needed me—"

"The same cunt who blew up our warehouses? You're rushing at his beck and call?"

"I did. Somebody tried to kill him, but he got the drop on them first. He needed somewhere secure to question him. How were we supposed to know the motherfucker was being tracked by the Chinese?"

"It doesn't even matter! You shouldn't have taken him there in the first place. Do you know how many weapons we lost? Thousands! They cleaned the warehouse out completely. I don't even want to tell you the dollar amount that we lost, because if I say it out loud, I might just rip your fucking head off."

"Are you done?"

"No, I'm not done. If you are going to be the one to lead us, you can't be making jackass decisions like that. It makes us look stupid and weak."

"Boogie—"

"Oh, shut up saying his name already. I don't even understand why we are working with him. One minute he's blowing our warehouses up, and the next minute we are in cahoots with him again."

"You wouldn't understand."

"What I understand is that Boogie and all the rest are going to be our downfall if we don't take hold of the reins now."

"What are you saying, Ella?"

"I'm saying I don't want to end up like *Papá*. If you aren't ready to lead and take over where he left off, then let Javier or Rafael take his place."

"You want our cousins to take over when I'm right here?"

"All I'm saying is that they're older and wise like our *papá*."

"I made one mistake. One! Nobody is going to take my father's place but me. It's my birthright."

"Then act like you give a damn about it. That's all I'm saying," Daniella said, and her eyes softened. "Lorenzo, *hermano,* this is not our war. Let's just let them fight it out and destroy each other. We'll be the last ones standing with high numbers. New York will be ours."

"That's not what *Papá* would do. He would stand beside Caesar. And Caesar is standing beside Boogie."

"Then I hope you don't die beside them as well." The fire returned to Daniella's eyes, and she stormed out of the shed.

"Yeah, me too," Zo said to himself before going back to work on the gun in his hands.

Chapter 25

Although Nicky had asked for half of the stash to be moved, Nathan felt that it would be wise to move the other half too. Just to be on the safe side. The laundromat had felt like the perfect hiding place at first. But it was also public knowledge that Caesar owned the business. Nathan didn't want to run the chance of it falling into Tao's hands. After what had happened the other night, none of them could be too careful. Word was Tao's men had completely cleaned out Marco's warehouse and taken all of the new shipments of guns and ammunition. That wasn't good for anybody. So far, the Chinese were up, and everyone else was just taking their blows.

Nathan was just glad he had somewhere off the radar to take the money. Years prior, Nathan thought he had fallen in love. It surprised the hell out of him since he was so shut off emotionally most times. But a woman named Janae stole his heart. She was a beautiful and thick chocolate drop with long hair and full lips. He didn't know if it was her personality or the way she could suck a mean dick that made him fall. Anything she wanted, she got. Nathan was so head over heels for Janae that he bought her a ring and a house in Jersey. However, shortly before he could present her with either, he got bumped up in a drop gone wrong. When he was shipped away to jail, Janae showed her real colors. While he was waiting for his lawyer to work his magic, Janae didn't visit him one time or answer one phone call. Not only that, she

156 C. N. Phillips

was slowly but surely cleaning out his bank account. She thought he was going away for a long time, so when he was released due to the police arresting him without a search warrant, she was in for a rude awakening. The only thing that saved her life from Nathan's wrath was that he did love her at one point, even though she ended up to be nothing but a gold digger. Long story short, Nathan kept the ring and the house. He never moved in and had been planning to sell it. However, now he had some use for it. Nobody knew it existed, not even his brother. Nathan was too ashamed to admit that he had ever been that pussy whipped by a bitch.

It was almost midnight by the time he got to the laundromat. It closed at eleven, so no one was inside. Nathan used a key to open the doors, and he didn't lock them again since he planned on coming back out to load the car. He made his way to the back and knocked on the locked door.

"Code," Ross's voice demanded from the other side of the door.

"It's me, fat ass," Nathan said and impatiently waited for Ross to open the door.

"Me who?" Ross asked.

"Nigga, don't play with me, I don't have time."

"I need the code, or I can't open the door for you," Ross said, and Nathan groaned.

He'd given Ross such a hard time about just opening the door that Nathan didn't realize that he'd forgotten the code word. He thought long and hard about what it could be but came up short. He hit the door again with his hand.

"Ross, just look through the peephole and see that it's me."

"I already see you, Nathan."

"Then open the door!"

"Is this a test or somethin'? Because I don't want to open it and you pistol whip me or somethin'."

"I'm gon' pistol whip you if you don't open this fuckin' door. Now!"

"A'ight, a'ight. No need to get your panties in a bunch," Ross told him, and Nathan heard the locks turning on the other side.

"Took you long enough." Nathan cut his eyes at Ross when the door swung open.

"Do you want me to follow your orders or not?"

"I want you to follow my orders until I tell you not to follow my orders. Move."

Nathan moved past him and headed down the stairs. He was met with the familiar sight of women in their bras packing up product. He didn't interrupt them from doing what they were doing, instead he went straight for the illusion wall. Two men named Bait and Raq stood holding AK-47s with their backs to it. They moved out of the way when they saw Nathan approaching. He slid the heavy wall over and revealed the vault behind it.

"I need all of this money bagged up in the next hour for transport," he told them after he unlocked the safe. "Put these bitches to work."

"Y'all heard the man. Bag this shit up!" Raq commanded, and the women instantly stopped doing what they were doing. There were duffle bags along one of the walls in the basement that were usually used to move product around. Each woman grabbed one and headed inside of the vault. As they passed, one of the women caught Nathan's attention.

"Janae?" he asked, surprised to see her.

Upon hearing her name, she turned a set of tired eyes to Nathan. She was still as pretty as he remembered, but still, she looked different. She was skinnier and looked like life had really worn her down. Once she recognized who he was, one of her hands flew to the disheveled wig on her head and tried to smooth it out.

"Nathan? What are you doin' here?"

"You know what I'm doin' here. Since when did you become a dope girl?" he asked, pointing at the gloves on her hands.

"Ever since I lost my job and needed the extra money. Workin' for Caesar has been keepin' me afloat. I never thought I would see you again. Not this close up, anyway. I heard you a big nigga now."

"Been a big nigga. You sure I can trust you around all this money?" He could tell his dig touched her, but he couldn't help it. Her standing right there in front of him opened wounds that weren't completely healed. The one thing he never understood was why she did him like that. She could have asked him for whatever she wanted and gotten it. Why did she have to steal from him?

"I apologized for that," she said.

"Did you? I vaguely remember you just gettin' your shit and bouncin'."

"You had a gun to my head! Do you remember that part?"

"Of course I do. I remember that I didn't pull the trigger. But we're talkin' about the fact that you never apologized."

"Maybe I didn't. But I always regretted doin' you like that, Nathan. You were good to me."

"I know I was. And you repaid me by bein' a low-down bitch."

"I deserve that." She nodded.

"Don't agree with me."

"Okay."

"Stop that!"

"What do you want me to do, Nathan? I can't take back the past."

"I just want you to tell me why."

"I . . . I don't know." Her palms faced the ceiling as she shrugged with sadness drenching her face. "I guess I was just scared."

"Scared of what?"

"That you were never comin' home. That I was gon' be alone. And I was mad at you for puttin' yourself in that situation. I don't know, Nathan. I was young and stupid. And when you gave me access to your accounts, I just helped myself. It was wrong. And I wish I could give you more than a sorry."

Nathan was still angry at her for what she did, but Janae looked so pitiful standing before him. There was no more point in verbally abusing her. She looked to be at her lowest. The old Janae would never even come out of the house if she wasn't in tip-top shape. The woman standing in front of him looked like a tattered version of her old self. He pointed to the other women stuffing their duffle bags with stacks of cash.

"Just get to work," he told her and turned away.

Rubbing his hands, he walked over to the tables the girls had been working on. They'd been in the middle of sewing bags of cocaine and pills inside the bag of dresses. He was about to weigh one of the Baggies to make sure that everything was adding up, but a thud on the upper level made him stop in his tracks. He looked at the ceiling and thought maybe Ross had fallen, but then he heard the sound of multiple sets of footsteps.

"Yo, you hear that?" Raq asked, coming to stand by Nathan.

"Yeah, I hear that shit," Nathan said, brandishing his gun. "Ain't nobody s'posed to be here but us. Stay down here. I'm about to go check on Ross's fat ass. Stay alert."

"You already know."

Nathan left them there and went to go check out what was happening on the top level. In his mind he pictured a bunch of Asian men running up in the laundromat ready to get things popping. It was almost a shame that that was what he was hoping for. He'd been itching for some action, and maybe that night he was finally going to get some.

"Ross?" he whispered loudly up the stairs. There was no answer, which was odd because Ross never left his post when he was on duty. "Shit!"

Pointing his gun and crouching slightly, Nathan carefully made his way up the stairs. When he got there, he saw that the door Ross was guarding stood wide open. That was the second red flag. The third was the voices he heard talking lowly in the laundromat. Nathan glanced down the stairs and thought to call for Bait and Raq, but they were too far. He said a quick prayer to his angels and prepared to smoke as many Asians as possible.

"Ahhh!" he shouted and rushed through the door with his finger on the trigger.

"Ay, whoa!"

Nathan registered the voice just in time as his brother's. Nicky had jumped back and was giving his brother a stare as if Nathan had gone off his rocker. Gun still raised, Nathan glanced quickly around the room. There weren't any Asians inside, just Caesar, Nicky, Ross, and a few goons standing watch at the door. When he realized that it was a false alarm, he let his arm drop to his side and wiped down on his face with his free hand.

"I'm *tellin'* y'all. You need to put this nigga on medicine!" Ross exclaimed, waving his hands at them as he walked away. "I'm goin' back to my post."

"What . . . what the fuck are y'all doin' here?" he asked, trying to slow his heart rate.

"I do believe I own this place, nephew. I can come any-time I want," Caesar said with a bewildered expression.

"I mean, what are y'all doin' here right now?"

"I could ask you the same question," Nicky said. "I thought you moved that money the other day."

"I did, but I thought it might be smart to just move the rest of it too," Nathan answered.

"That's actually why we're here. Not only that, but Caesar wants to close shop at this location permanently."

"Why? What's goin' on?"

"I heard about what happened at Marco's warehouse. I can't risk taking a loss like that," Caesar said. "And after what happened to Stefano—"

"That Italian motherfucka? What happened to him?"

"He was found dead in his pizzeria. I thought it was Boogie's doing since I knew there was tension between him and the Italians ever since he took over."

"It wasn't him?"

"Stefano and two other men were found with knives lodged in their bodies. Kunai knives."

"Damn, the Chinese got to him too?"

"It seems that way," Caesar said with a sigh. "I don't know what all Tao knows about my operation, but I need to switch everything up."

"You know we got you, Unc."

"Where were you planning on relocating the money to?" Nicky asked his brother.

"My place."

"The condo?"

"Nah, my house in Jersey." Nathan tried to say it as casually as possible, but it didn't go over Nicky's head.

"House? When did you buy one of those?"

"Damn, a nigga can't have a house? I might want a family one day."

"I don't know what's confusing me more—that you have a house or that you're talking about having a fam."

"Man, let's just worry about movin' the loot. The girls are baggin' the shit up right now."

"Good. We have a van waiting outside," Caesar said. "When you're done, go home and get some rest. We have a long few days ahead of us. And with any luck, we'll make it out alive."

The night was still as Ming sat outside a nice distance away from the laundromat. He was parked in a stolen Ford Taurus away from the streetlights and shadowed by darkness. In his lap he had pictures of Caesar and the two men with him. He learned they were his nephews Nathan and Nicky. Nicky was set to take over for Caesar if anything happened to him, but at the moment he was his distro. Nathan was the muscle. He looked from the pictures to the men outside in the parking lot of the laundromat, and they matched up with the photos he had on his lap. He watched as Caesar and others loaded a van with black duffel bags. There could be only one of two things inside of them: money or drugs. Ming was far enough away to not be noticed but close enough to hear some of what was being said.

"A'ight. I'ma drop this and meet y'all out there," Nathan said.

"You're not going with them?" Nicky asked, pointing to the men preparing to drive off in the van.

"Nah, I have some business to handle real quick."

Nathan glanced down the street and rubbed the top of his head. Ming remained still in the car, even though he was certain Nathan couldn't see him.

"That's cool." Nicky nodded. "I'ma see you though, bro."

The two men slapped hands and embraced. Nicky got in the car with Caesar, and Nathan went back inside of the laundromat. Ming had been following Caesar around the entire day and he battled with himself over whether he should continue following him or go after Nathan. He didn't seem to have any security around him, and Ming knew it would be too easy. He lay back in his seat when the van drove by and stayed low when Caesar's Rolls-Royce followed soon after. He decided to just stay on course and follow Caesar. He sat up and prepared to start the car, but as soon as he put the key in the ignition, the glass on the driver side window shattered suddenly.

"I thought I saw a chink spyin' on us!" Nathan's voice growled.

He reached in, unlocked the door, and yanked Ming out of the car. His fist quickly found Ming's jaw, sending him flying to the ground. Ming tried to go for the knives on his belt, but Nathan ran and kicked him in the mouth.

"Oh, no you don't! I heard how you get down with the knives. Unfortunately for you, I don't like getting cut."

Every time he tried to get up, Nathan knocked him back down. The blood in his mouth tasted salty, and as Nathan commenced beating him to a pulp, he felt his eyes begin to swell. He was beaten until his entire body was numb. He had never felt searing pain like that before. Ming had never been caught off guard, but there was a first time for everything, and it was a humbling experience. When Nathan was done having his fun with his fists, he pulled out his pistol.

"Just kill me," Ming murmured weakly, hoping for a quick death.

"You wish. As much as it would pleasure me to watch the blood spill out of your body, I'm not gon' shoot yo' sorry ass. I'm gon' let Caesar handle you." On his last word, Nathan smashed a gun on the side of Ming's head, knocking him out cold.

Chapter 26

"Mmmm."

Ming's groan as he regained consciousness was due to the pain that suddenly swept through his body. He ached everywhere, especially the side of his head. He tried to reach for his forehead but found that his arm would not move. He opened his eyes and looked down, seeing a tight rope around his right wrist. Looking at the left and then at both of his ankles, he saw the same thing. At first confusion filled him, but then his memory came back: Caesar, the laundromat, and Nathan beating him up. He'd been captured. How had he let himself get captured? His father would be angry. So very angry. Ming's training began when he was just a boy. His father started him so young to avoid that kind of thing. Nathan had to have moved with the stealth of a leopard for Ming not to have noticed him getting close to the car.

Letting his eyes get used to the sunlight beaming through a window on his far right, he blinked feverishly. When his sight was no longer blurry, he peered around the room that he was in. It was obvious by the shelves of books that he was in some sort of library. The chair he was bound to was dead in the center of the room, facing the door.

"The guest of honor is finally awake," a voice to the left of him said.

He did not know the deep baritone voice. He turned his head to the direction of the person who spoke, and he saw a man sitting there wearing a designer suit while casually sipping a cup of tea. Everything about his demeanor read relaxed and unbothered. Caesar King was an undaunted man, and the two of them were alone in the library.

"Where am I?"

"I guess it might be hard to recognize this place on the inside since the last time you saw it you were aiming guns at it."

When he said that, Ming knew he was talking about the Big House. It was a place that only the heads of each family were supposed to know about, but before his uncle Li died, he told Tao where it was. The thing that Caesar didn't know was that Boogie saved his life by killing Li. Because if he hadn't been murdered, then Caesar would have been killed on Li's command. Li not only told his nephew about the house's existence, but also that Caesar was a sitting duck inside. It was a small victory for Boogie and Caesar, but it only prolonged the inevitable, which was accepting Tao's rule.

"Are you the man who killed my uncle?" Ming's voice was barely audible, but it carried in the silence of the room.

"Li? No, I did not."

"I know who killed him. I am speaking about Shen."

"Li's other nephew. I have no idea what you're talking about. But if he is dead, I'm not sorry about it. You should know as well as I do that casualties and wars spare no favorites."

Caesar seemed like a man who would own up to anything he did. But Ming still didn't let him off the hook. He may not have been the one who physically killed Shen, but it still could have been somebody in his camp.

"We shall find out soon enough if you did it. But if you did, I hope you have a burial plot picked out . . . if they find your body, that is."

"It's always funny when the men at my mercy make threats." Caesar's smirk showed that he wasn't affected by Ming's words.

"Why did your hound not kill me? He had the perfect opportunity to."

"You mean my nephew. And he didn't kill you because why would we kill our most precious bargaining tool?"

"I should have figured. You're going to use me to get to my father."

"Of course we are. And torture you a little bit. Have you ever been tortured before?"

"Try as you might, I won't tell you anything."

"You just haven't felt the kind of pain that will make you tell me everything," Caesar said, placing the teacup on the desktop. He got up and came in front of Ming, kneeling so the two of them were at eye level. "First, I'm going to starve you. You'll be so hungry and thirsty you won't know which way is right or left. And then I'm going to cut off your toes one by one. I guarantee by the third toe you'll be singing like a canary."

"What is it that you want to know so badly?"

"Everything that I don't know about your father and his operation. And you're going to tell me."

Caesar sounded confident, and he looked it, too. He just knew that he would be able to break Ming. But he had no idea what Tao put him through to be the murderous killer he'd grown into. To Caesar's words, Ming smiled, confusing him.

"Once, when I was just ten years old," Ming started, "I missed a step while training blindfolded with my father. I was carrying a heavy bucket of water up a concrete flight of stairs. But I tripped before I made it to the top. He whipped the bottom of my feet so badly that I had bloody gashes. He did that every single time until I made it to the top step with the water. And even after I made it, he whipped me for not getting it right the first time. And there was another time I lost a fighting match to a boy much bigger than me. My father did not feed me for ten days. Also, starting at age fifteen, once a week I lay on hot stones to grow familiar with the feeling of torment. So, Caesar, I can go on and on about the things my father did to me, all to say that I am no stranger to pain. I was trained with it. Do your worst. I will still tell you nothing."

Caesar's jaw tightened, and a vein popped out from his temple. He said nothing, which pleased Ming. Caesar's face was expressionless as he stared at his hostage. Suddenly, he gave a small laugh and left Ming alone in the library.

Used to spending long durations deep in meditation, Ming used his time bound to explore his own mind. He didn't know how long he'd been knocked out before he came around, but he was sure it couldn't have been longer than a day. His head hung with his chin to his chest, and he wondered if his father had begun searching for him. It wasn't uncommon for Ming to go off on his own for a few days. However, he always checked in.

Hours passed before the door opened again. Expecting Caesar to step inside the library, Ming was surprised to see a young, pretty woman. Her brown skin glistened in the sunlight as she walked toward him, holding a tray. She placed it down on a table and hurried back to the door. She glanced out skittishly before quietly shutting it.

"Are you hungry?" she asked him with concern in her voice.

Picking a plate up off the tray, Ming saw there was a sandwich on top of it. She got close to him and held it up to his mouth, but he turned his head.

"You're trying to poison me," he told her.

"Poison?" She sounded offended. "I just thought you would be hungry. I came here with my daddy today, and when I found out he had you locked up here, I—"

"Your father? Caesar?"

"Yes," she said.

"I should have known. You have his eyes. Yours are . . . soft."

"I've heard that once or twice," she said and sighed, looking at Ming in his beaten-up state. "Most times I don't agree with the things he does. It isn't right."

"Most times?"

"I'm not naive. I know the business my daddy is in. He's never tried to hide it. And I know sometimes things are necessary. But I don't know about this. This war with the Chinese just seems so hasty. Our families have coexisted for so long."

"Caesar made the decision to side with our enemy. So that makes him the enemy."

"I guess. I guess I understand why you're tied up then," she said sadly.

"What is your name?"

"Amelia. But you can call me Milli."

"Milli," he repeated.

"Yes. Now that you know my name, what's yours?"

"Ming."

"Ming?" She made a face. "That's a different name."

"So is Milli."

"I guess you're right. Anyway, my dad said he's not going to feed you for a long time. So I suggest you eat now and preserve your strength."

She held up the sandwich again, and Ming surveyed it. He didn't know if he could trust her. Actually, of course he knew he couldn't trust her. But her face was kind. And she was right. If he was going to withstand the wrath of Caesar King, he needed to keep his strength up. He opened his mouth and took a bite. It wasn't bad at all. He hadn't eaten a ham and cheese sandwich since he was a child. He took another bite, and then another.

"You were hungry," Milli noted when the sandwich was gone.

"Do you have something to drink?" Ming asked, feeling the dryness of his mouth.

"Yes. Water. But I don't suggest you drink too much. My dad isn't going to let you use the restroom," she said and grabbed a water bottle from the tray. She opened it, held it to his lips, and let him take a few gulps. "Ming? Are you a bad man?"

"You might think so," he answered once he was done washing the food down.

"You don't know what I might think. Have you killed before?"

"Yes."

"Many people?"

"More than I can remember."

"I guess it just depends on the reasons why."

"Sometimes for no reason at all," Ming told her.

"Why?"

"Because my father orders me to," Ming said, but he didn't know why he told her that, even though it was the truth.

"Orders you to? You say that like you're a soldier or something."

"I guess you can say that I am his soldier. He has many enemies, including your father."

"Then I guess I know why my dad doesn't plan on letting you go anytime soon. I just wish that all of this feuding would stop and things would go back to normal."

"When my father is finished with yours, the normal you're used to will be a thing of the past."

"You say that like my dad is going to lose this war."

"He is."

"Then you don't know Caesar King."

"I don't need to know him to tell you my father is going to defeat him. When he dies, he's going to lose everybody he loves at the same time. Including you."

His stare was so cold that Milli's skin got goosebumps. She stepped away from him with the bottle of water in her hand and left him alone again.

Chapter 27

I make shit shake, up in broad day
No face, ain't no case, learned that the hard way
King Von's voice, along with the vibration of the bass in Boogie's car, made his head nod along with the beat. He pulled into his driveway next to Roz's car and turned off the car. He was about to get out, but then his phone rang. He looked down and saw that it was Diana.

"Hello?"

"Boogie, I need to talk to you immediately."

"Is everything good? You sound tense."

"Because I am. How soon can you meet me at the Sugar Trap?"

"Wait, you're at the Sugar Trap? I thought you were still takin' it easy."

"How easy can I take it when you were almost killed outside of my house?"

"We handled that. Well, kind of. Anyways, what are you doin' at the Sugar Trap?"

"It's sounding like you're forgetting it's my business in the first place."

"No, I'm—"

"Afraid I might find out what you've been doing in my absence? Just get your ass down here."

"A'ight. I'll be there in an hour."

When the two of them disconnected, Boogie stared at the steering wheel of his car. Diana's words and tone played again in his head, and he knew that whatever she wanted wasn't going to be pleasant for him. He gave a small groan and got out of the car. He was hoping to spend a little more than an hour with Roz and Amber, but they would have to understand.

"Baby?" he called when he opened the front door and stepped inside.

The entire house was spotless, not one toy in sight. It was quiet, almost like nobody was home, even though he'd seen Roz's car. But he knew how the house sounded during the day when Amber was awake. She was always into something, and when she heard the front door open, she usually ran to find him.

"Baby?" he called again. "Amber?"

Still there was no answer. He went toward their bedrooms and could hear someone moving around in the master room. Instinctively his hand rested on his gun as he inched toward the slightly closed door. He pushed it open slowly with one hand and saw something that made his heart drop to his stomach.

"Roz, what's this?"

Roz stopped doing what she was doing and looked at Boogie standing in the doorway. She was holding a handful of clothes over a suitcase. From the looks of it, she was almost done. When she saw Boogie standing there, a look of guilt flashed across her face. She didn't say anything to him. She just stuffed what was in her hands into the suitcase and zipped it shut.

"Where are you goin'?" he asked.

"I'm leaving, Boogie."

"Leavin'? You mean for the weekend?"

"No, I'm leaving until I can figure out if this is something that I really can do." She looked up at the ceiling and sighed. "I thought I could do it. I really did, but . . ."

"But what?" Boogie went and stood in front of her. "What has you wantin' to just up and leave me? And where's Amber?"

"She's at my friend's house. That's where we'll be staying."

"Roz, you can't be serious." Boogie tried to make her look at him, but she pulled away. "Roz . . ."

"You know, I can't remember the last time we made love."

"We fuck all the time!" Boogie exclaimed.

"Exactly, nigga! You 'fuck' me. Quickies! That's all you have time for these days. You haven't made *love* to me in forever. I'm up all hours of the night hopin' and prayin' you make it back home."

"You knew what you signed up for when you started fuckin' with me. I'm in the streets regulatin' and makin' sure we eat! And there's a lot of shit I still gotta make up for. I don't like it either, but it has to be done."

"Does it? Or is that what you tell yourself?"

"Roz, who are you right now?" Boogie asked, making a face. "You're actin' like you don't know me. Talk to me."

Roz plopped down on their bed and covered her eyes with her hand. Boogie could tell by the way her chest bounced that she'd begun to cry. Her lips quivered when she inhaled and removed her hand from her face. She turned her gaze back to him and allowed her tears to fall freely. That time when her gaze fell on him, he saw something different in her eyes. He saw hostility.

"How am I supposed to believe Amber and I will be safe when you can't even protect the niggas closest to you?"

There it was. The elephant in the room. The two of them hadn't really talked about Gino's death. He just figured he was dealing with it in his way, and she was dealing with it in hers. Her words hit him so hard that it felt like someone had really punched him in the chest, mainly because he blamed himself for Gino getting caught lacking the way he had been. He shouldn't have sent him off alone. Gino should have had at least three shooters with him. But Boogie had underestimated the enemy.

"What happened to Gino is fucked up. Me and Bentley—"

"And that's another thing! Have you even thought to ask my brother how he's doin'? His cousin just was killed, and you have him runnin' around like a fuckin' robot!"

"Gino dyin' doesn't change the fact that shit needs to be done. Bentley knows that and is doin' what he has to do!"

"Yeah, to keep himself busy. He was close to Gino. You would see how much he's hurtin' if you had been at the funeral."

"It's fucked up. It's all fucked up," Boogie told her.

"Fucked up is an understatement. He's dead. Dead and never coming back. Dead because of . . ." She stopped.

"Say it. Say what you were gon' say."

"Boogie . . ."

"He's dead because of me."

"I didn't mean to say it like that."

"Then how did you mean it?" Boogie looked at her, but she didn't say anything. He stepped away from her and motioned at the door. "A'ight. Go."

"Boogie . . ."

"Nah. You feel like you aren't safe, remember? And if I can't protect you, then there's not a point in you bein' around me. Get out!"

His deep shout made Roz jump. He'd never spoken to her like that before. Her eyes were swimming in tears in seconds, but he had become too angry to care. She wanted to leave him instead of remaining solid by his side. She grabbed her suitcase and walked out of the room. Boogie ignored the twisting of his heart when he heard the front door slam.

Chapter 28

Milli left the library feeling chills. She never put herself in her father's business because it never felt like it was her place. And talking to Ming was a good reason why. He scared her. It was the nothing in his eyes that did it. He was empty. If Milli didn't know anything else, she knew Ming was a cold-blooded killer. She let her head fall back as her hand wrapped tightly around the water bottle in her hands. She found herself wondering if the ties on Ming's hands and ankles were even enough to hold him. Glancing back at the library door, she held her breath, half expecting it to burst open, but it didn't. She stood up straight again and went down the staircase to the first level of the house. She stopped in the study and found Caesar standing next to the fireplace. When he saw that she'd entered the room, the first thing he noticed was the spooked look on her face.

"What happened?" he asked.

"He's crazy," was all she said.

She placed the water bottle in her hand on a coffee table and sat down in one of the brown leather chairs. Caesar stared at the partially drunk water bottle and then at his daughter. He came and knelt in front of her.

"What did you find out?" His eyes locked on hers.

"Daddy, I . . ." Milli started, but then she saw the eager look on her father's face. She knew she was about to disappoint him. "Nothing really."

She thought he was about to be let down, but if he was, he didn't show it. He stood back up and resumed his stance by the fireplace. His brow furrowed like he was lost in thought. The room was quiet for a while before he finally spoke again.

"I sent you in there because I thought he might trust your innocence in all of this."

"I'm sorry. I let you down, Daddy."

"Never. I should have known that someone with his skill set wouldn't be broken with a sandwich and water bottle," he said, huffing out a breath.

"What are you going to do now?"

"I don't know. But whatever it is, you don't have to worry your pretty little head with it."

"I'm not a child, Daddy," she said.

"I know. But I never want to see you looking how you looked when you walked in this study. You were almost pale. What happened in there?"

"I just . . . I'm around dangerous men all the time. But Ming? He gives me chills. He said that when you die, everyone you love will die at the same time. Including me."

"Is that what scared you?"

"No, it's that he meant it. The way he looked when he said it was like it was already set in stone."

"Well, I'll be the first to tell you that many men have tried and failed at killing me. Ming and his father are just the next in line. Don't let those words get to you. Matter of fact, forget you even met a scum like him."

She nodded her head but started to blink feverishly. Tears had sprung quickly to her eyes, and she felt so many emotions in her chest. Milli normally wasn't such an emotional person. In fact, in many ways she was very much like her father. Before one tear could drop, Caesar was by her side with a hand around her shoulder. He held her without saying anything. He just rocked her side to side like he would do when she was upset as a child. She waited for the lump to leave her throat to talk.

"I just don't want to lose you again, Daddy," she said in a voice barely above a whisper. "When I thought you were dead, it showed me how unprepared I was to really lose you. I was lost. My heart was broken, and I don't even know if it's all the way back together yet."

"Why do you think that is?"

"My entire life, I went without seeing you hurt. Not once. I guess I always thought you were invincible like Superman. But this . . . this showed me that you're just a man. An extraordinary man, but you bleed just like the rest of them."

"That's why I've always made sure to be smarter than the rest of them. Rest assured, baby girl, that when it's my time to go, it won't be at the hands of someone else. I've given the game so much that I've been blessed to have a full life. I plan to be around to see my grandkids, but don't move too quick on that one."

His words made Milli smile, and that in turn made him smile. She buried her face in his chest and inhaled his cologne. Although her emotions weren't completely at rest, she did feel a little bit better. He wiped the water from her cheeks and kissed her forehead.

"I love you, Daddy," she told him.

"I love you too, baby girl."

Knock! Knock!

The two of them turned to see Nicky standing in the entry way to the study. He had an apologetic look on his face when he saw that he had interrupted them. He had a piece of paper in his hands that he held up for Caesar to see.

"What is that?"

"The flyers for the block party on Saturday. They've been putting them around the city all week. Everywhere I go, I see one of these stapled or taped to something."

"Daddy, are you sure you're up for all of that?" Milli asked, concerned.

"As ready as I'll ever be. I've barely showed my face since I've been back."

"Yeah, don't worry about Unc." Nicky grinned at her. "This will send a good message to the boys who look up to him in the streets."

"And to the ones who don't, it will show them what resilience looks like. Manhattan is still mine. I bleed these streets, and no one is going to take them from me."

"We'll double the security all around the block just in case anyone thinks that they're gon' come in and do anything stupid. You're a very powerful man, Unc. And this 'coming back from the dead' shit has made you more popular than you know. Nathan said he wants to be your personal bodyguard during the event."

"I can't think of anybody else for the job." Caesar nodded. "There's only one thing left to do before then."

"What?" both Nicky and Milli asked in unison.

"Set up a meeting with Tao."

Chapter 29

When Boogie got to the Sugar Trap, he didn't go in right away. He lingered in the parking lot and went to the spot where Gino was murdered. It wasn't hard to find. Although someone had come and tried to scrub all of the blood up, there was still some left. Boogie couldn't help but think about what a horrible way to die that was. The funeral had been a small going-away service, and he, of course, paid for everything. It was quick, the way Gino would've liked it. Roz was wrong by thinking Boogie wasn't there. He was. However, he'd sat in the back. He couldn't face Gino's mother, knowing that Gino died going on a mission for him. He knelt down and thought back to the moments right before Gino was murdered.

"Gino! What the hell are you doin', man?" Boogie *shouted over the loud music in the Sugar Trap.*

Gino was sitting in one of the private sections as women shook their asses all around him unapologetically. He was grabbing big handfuls of them and making biting motions with his teeth. It was obvious that he was enjoying himself thoroughly. Boogie's voice had been serious, but he wanted to laugh at the same time as he watched the scene unfold.

"I'm enjoyin' these hoes! What does it look like I'm doin'?"

"Diana would bust a cap in that ass if she heard you call 'em hoes."

"My bad, sluts!"

"Ay, chill out," Boogie said and then turned to one of the girls. "Earthquake, right?"

She stopped what she was doing the moment Boogie spoke to her. She seemed to be both shocked and excited that he had addressed her. She walked seductively over to him and tried to take his hand and pull him into the section, but he shook his head.

"Not that kind of party," he said.

"Yeah, Boogie is a damn near married man. Ain't that right, boss?" Gino said with his eyes still on a woman bent over in front of him.

"Damn," Earthquake said and licked her luscious lips. "I've been waiting on the day I can give you a spin ever since you've been running things for the boss lady. The streets are calling your name loud as a motherfucker. And you're fine as hell. You sure I can't take you to the Paradise Room real quick?"

"I'm straight on that," Boogie said, dismissing her advance. "I do have a question for you though."

"Talk to me, baby."

"Have you seen another girl who works here, named Desire?" The moment the words were out of his mouth, Earthquake rolled her eyes.

"Oh, you mean Miss Thing. The one who thinks she's better than everybody because you trusted her with something important? That Desire?"

"Yeah. That Desire."

"I haven't seen her in . . . it's been a few days. Damn, now that I think about it, Desire never misses work. Maybe she's sick or something. This is her address and phone number if you want to check up on her." She wrote the information down on a napkin with a pen she found on the table and handed it to him.

"Maybe. . . ." Boogie let his voice trail off as he took the napkin. He turned to Gino and hit him in the shoulder. "Ay, let me talk to you for a second."

"*Right now?*"

"*Yeah, nigga. Right now. You ain't payin' no way.*"

"*I'll be back, ladies,*" *Gino assured them, but Boogie shook his head.*

"*No, he won't. Go make some real money. Don't y'all got dues to pay soon?*"

The women stopped dancing and scrambled away. Boogie stepped in the section and sat across from Gino, ignoring Earthquake as she gave him one last seductive look before she too walked away.

"*Damn! I see why they call that bitch Earthquake. That booty is amazin'!*"

"*What I miss?*" *Bentley's voice sounded as he joined them in the VIP section, sitting next to Gino.*

"*Nothin', just your cousin bein' thirsty as fuck,*" *Boogie said, shaking his head.*

"*Damn, cuz. You act like you don't get no pussy,*" *Bentley said and laughed.*

"*Nigga, you saw that ass on that bitch. You would fuck it too.*"

Bentley glanced at Earthquake from where he sat as she bent over and twerked in front of a man at a table. A smile crossed his face as he watched her butt and thighs ripple.

"*I might,*" *he said, and the two of them shared a laugh.*

"*I'm glad the two of you are enjoyin' yourselves, but we need to talk about somethin' a little more serious.*"

"*What's good, G?*"

"*Desire's missin',*" *Boogie said.*

"*Who is Desire?*" *Gino asked with a confused look on his face. "You cheatin' on Roz?*"

"*No, stupid ass! Desire is a girl who works here. I kind of sent her on a job for me.*"

"*She's the one you sent to meet with that Chinese motherfucka, ain't it?*"

"Yup. She was supposed to check in days ago. But I haven't heard from her. I thought I would find her here."

"Hold up, run that shit back. Why the hell would you send someone to meet with the Chinese? A stripper at that." Gino was growing more and more confused by the second.

"Tao's brother Shen reached out to me. He was a regular here before all of this shit started. There was nowhere that the two of us could meet, so I figured out another way to pass the information. I thought it was foolproof, but apparently not."

"What did he want to tell you?"

"Somethin' on Tao. It had to have been pretty important, too. I won't know what it is though until I find her."

"Earthquake just gave you the information on where Desire lives, so maybe somebody needs to do a pop up." Gino spoke the words, but both Boogie and Bentley looked at him. "Me? Y'all want me to do it?"

"I told Roz I would be home a little earlier tonight."

"And shit, I just don't want to." Bentley shrugged his shoulders. "I've been in the field all day. I need some sleep."

"You niggas are treatin' me like the annoyin' little brother right now."

"Can you go check or no? If not, I'll pull up," Boogie said, holding up the napkin.

"Nah, you go home to wifey," Gino said and took the paper. "I'll go check it out. And I'ma call you with the info."

Boogie snapped out of his memory and opened his eyes. He'd only known Gino for a short period of time, but time recently seemed so fluid that it felt like forever. He had a moment of silence for his lost brother before deciding to go inside the club.

Boogie stood up and noticed that there had been extra security cameras put in place all around the building. He also noticed that there were more lights in the parking lot. It was daytime, so they were not on. However, he knew those poles hadn't been there before. Diana was back calling the shots, and there was no doubt in his mind that Gino's death on her property was what prompted those changes. He went inside the Sugar Trap, and as soon as he stepped inside, Diana's girls flocked his way. Earthquake led the way. She was wearing a purple number with a matching G-string. Her hair was pulled up into a ponytail, and she had so much makeup on that Boogie wondered what she really looked like. They smiled big at him like he was made of a million bucks. Boogie wasn't a flashy man. He wore a watch and sometimes a chain, but he didn't walk around looking like money all the time. However, when everyone knew who you were, you didn't have to do all of that.

"Boogie, I didn't think I was going to be seeing you around here anymore now that Diana's back." Earthquake stuck her bottom lip out.

"I was kind of sad too. I was going to miss all that chocolate," the woman next to her said.

Boogie had come to know her by her stage name, Cheshire. Her smile was big, but her backside was bigger. She, like Earthquake, was always looking for a way to get in his pants. Mostly his pockets. Their hands were all over him, and they tried to lead him to a section. Boogie had never been the type to be moved by the allure of just any woman. To him, if the pussy was that easy, then he would never want it. He removed their hands from his body.

"I'm flattered, ladies, but I'm here for business, not pleasure. And from the looks of it, y'all should be busy instead of over here in my face. I know Diana will have a fit if she sees how you are movin' right now," Boogie said and pointed out all the paying customers inside the Sugar Trap sitting alone with no entertainment.

At the mention of Diana's name, the girls groaned.

"We liked when you were running the place," Earthquake whined.

"The thing about that is this was never my place. I was always temporary here. But even if I weren't, I would never be okay with y'all being this thirsty. Get to work."

They pursed their lips but didn't say another word as they walked away and left him to go find Diana. He walked down the hallway to Diana's office and wondered what that putrid smell was. Whatever it was, he knew he wasn't the only one who smelled it because he walked past several cleaning ladies scrubbing the floors and the walls.

Knock knock!

"Anybody in here?" Boogie asked as he poked his head in the door.

Diana was sitting by her desk, and upon seeing him, she frowned. That was all it took for Boogie to know that something wasn't right. Diana was always happy to see him even when she wasn't in a good mood.

"Come here and sit down. Shut the door."

Boogie did as she asked and noticed that when he stepped inside of her office the smell was worse. He didn't know how she was just sitting there basking in it, because he wanted to throw up. He walked to the desk and sat in the seat across from her, taking in her death stare.

"Did I forget to tell the cooks to clean the kitchen or something?" Boogie asked, half joking.

But Diana didn't laugh. In fact, she didn't so much as crack a smile. It was obvious that she didn't find anything funny. She continued to stare at him for a few moments before she finally tapped her finger on the desk three times.

"What have you been doing here in my absence?" she asked.

"I've been running shit like you want it."

"It seems to me like you've been doing a little bit more than that."

"You have to be a little less vague with me, Diana. You've always been direct. Don't make now any different."

"You've got a smart mouth just like your father did," Diana said, shaking her head. "I used to think it was cute, but right now I'm trying so hard not to slap the shit out of you."

"I'd rather you do that than beat around the bush."

"Fine. Why the hell would you send Desire alone to meet with that Chinese motherfucker?"

"How did you—"

"Because those bastards shipped her here in a fucking crate. You don't smell that? It's Desire."

"Damn. Diana, I am so sorry."

"'Sorry' won't bring her back. And 'sorry' won't change the fact that you made a decision without me. What were you thinking?"

"I don't know. The cat called me one night when I was chilling at home with the family."

"Who called you?"

"Shen Zhang."

"Tao's brother?"

"Yes. I don't know how he got my number or why, but the way he talked to me . . . I didn't think he was like the others. He told me he had some information about Tao that would change everything. But he couldn't tell me over the phone. He wanted to show me somethin'. I guess I trusted him because I wanted to believe in anything to get us all out of this mess. We're in this war because of me. That alone will be the elephant in the room until I figure the shit out."

Diana's eyes grew soft. He could tell that she was still mad, probably about the loss of one of her girls. But she didn't look like she wanted to kill him as much anymore.

"I just wish you'd told me."

"You were busy healin' and getting to know Morgan. I didn't wanna worry you with work."

"I'm always worried with work. Don't you understand? This is my life. I breathe this. From now on I need to know every call, every move, every play. Do you understand?"

"I understand," Boogie grumbled even though he felt like he was being chastised like a child. Suddenly he hit the top of the desk. "Damn, here I am thinking I'm a good judge of character, and I got somebody else killed. I didn't mean for Desire to die."

"That's the thing. Here I am telling Morgan that she needs to keep her ear to the streets, but I haven't heard one of the biggest things that happened. It took for Alex to tell me."

"Tell you what?"

"You don't know?"

"No." Boogie shook his head.

"He's dead. The man who called you? Shen? He's dead. They're trying to blame either you or Caesar's camp. I have to ask, did you have anything to do with it?"

"What? No! I didn't even know he was dead. But if he is, I highly doubt it was because of us."

"Then who?"

"What would you do if you found out somebody in your camp was plottin' to turn on you? And tryin'a give the enemy information that might destroy you?"

"I would kill him."

"Exactly. Me too. But I didn't."

"It was Tao."

"I'm thinkin' the same thing."

"I think you should take some time and look more into it. If there's one thing I know, it's that the Chinese take shit like that very seriously. And if Tao is responsible for killing his own brother, he has to be afraid that somebody will find out. Otherwise, why would he be covering it up?"

"Okay, I'll get right on it," Boogie said and sat there in silence.

Even though he wasn't looking at her, he could feel Diana's eyes watching him closely. That was why he tried to put Roz to the back of his mind, because he knew if he thought about her, it would read all over his face. Too late. It already did.

"What's on your mind, Boogie?"

"Nothing."

"Your father used to lie to me too when he didn't want to talk about something. I would give you a penny for your thoughts, but I'm not giving you shit. You got one of my girls killed, so talk."

"If you must know, Roz left." Boogie took a deep breath and let it out.

"As in packed her things and left?"

"Well, half left and half I told her to leave."

"Why?"

"All of this shit is just gettin' too heavy for her. You know Gino was her cousin. It just hit too close to home for her I guess."

"A death in the family does hit hard, especially when it's rare. I can tell just by being around Bentley that their blood is tough. And I'm not going to lie—after hearing that somebody was killed in my parking lot, it makes me look at the Chinese a lot differently. They're strong and fearless."

"And that's the other thing. Roz doesn't think she's safe."

"And what do you think?"

"I feel like I would fight a hundred men to keep my family safe. I could even be with her day and night nonstop. But this shit with Gino taught me that anybody can be touched, so I think she's right. Right now while shit is comin' at us from all sides, I think it's best she be somewhere else. Somewhere that I don't even know. And when it's over, we can get back on track."

"That's the thing, my dear Boogie. It will never be over. So if she can't handle it now at the beginning of your reign, then she'll never be able to handle it. And unfortunately that means she isn't the girl for you."

The words she'd spoken were the same words he'd been juggling in his own mind since he'd left home. It hit differently hearing them out loud. He wished they weren't true, but no matter how he tried to fight it, he knew Diana was right. He was who he was, and he wasn't falling back from the game anytime soon. It was just the beginning. So if Roz couldn't get with the program, then she never would.

"I don't know," he finally said and shrugged his shoulder. "I gotta take it a day at a time. But on another note, Diana?"

"Hmm?"

"Do you think that you could get me Desire's appointment book?" he asked.

He'd learned about the appointment book by working there. Some of the girls had one. It was how they kept track of their client meetups outside of the Sugar Trap. Only a few of the girls had the privilege to do so, and Desire was one of them.

"Sure. What for?" Diana's voice was curious.

"I think maybe I should drop in on the crime scene."

Chapter 30

All eyes were on the black fleet vehicle that transported Tao and his men through the streets of the Bronx. Tao ignored them. He adjusted the dark shades he wore over his eyes and focused on the phone in his hands. He went to the text message thread between himself and Ming to see if his son had tried to contact him. Still, there was nothing. It had been days since he had last seen or spoken to Ming, and he was wondering exactly what his son was up to. Chu On had been asking questions about why he hadn't seen him around the house, and Tao was running out of excuses. The last thing he needed was for Chu On to think something was wrong and withdraw his army from Tao. He hoped to hear from Ming soon, not because he was worried about him, but because there were jobs that needed to be done. Boogie was still moving around carefree, and Tao wanted him ended as soon as possible. And Caesar right after.

Tao had to admit he was shocked when he learned Caesar wanted to meet. At first it seemed like the perfect opportunity to kill him, but Caesar was too smart for his own good. He wanted to meet in a public place, so he chose the most public place of all: the Diamond Museum. The name described the museum exactly. It was a museum of the most expensive and rare diamonds from all over the world. And as one could assume, it was heavily guarded. There was no way Tao would be able to make a move on Caesar there. There was also no way that

Tao could bring all of his shooters inside. Both he and
Caesar agreed to only bring two people each with them.
Tao would normally have Ming by his side, but instead he
had two of his well-trained younger cousins, Jin and Lan,
with him. They were just as deadly as his son. However,
Tao didn't know them. They were being loaned to him on
Chu On's orders. The two of them sat quietly in the back
seat of the Bentley truck the entire ride.

When they got there, Tao peered outside of the window.
Although it was a weekday, tourists kept the museum
very busy. Tao's driver pulled into one of the parking
garages and dropped them off at the door before he
parked nearby. Tao walked with Jin in the front, and
Lan covered his six. The building was busy already,
and when they reached the entrance to the museum,
Tao thought the metal detectors were going to be an
issue, since they all were armed. But luck was on their
side. Standing there manning the metal detector wasn't
just any security guard. He was Chinese. Upon seeing
Tao, recognition struck him, and he even stood a little
straighter. Discreetly, he waved him through the other
door, which didn't have a metal detector. The moment
they were through, Tao's phone rang.

"Hello?"

"Come downstairs to the blood diamonds exhibit. I am
by the waterfall."

Click.

They found the escalator that took them to the lower
level of the museum, and Tao could hear the waterfall
before he saw it. It was a little ways away from the
entrance of the exhibit, and there was a table in front of
it. Tao saw Caesar already seated and waiting patiently.
Standing with their backs to the water fountain and
facing the table were two black men who Tao could only
guess were Caesar's security. He walked over to the table,

and Caesar got up from his chair. He gave a small nod to acknowledge Tao, and Tao repeated the gesture. Lan pulled his chair out for him before he and Jin stood to the side by the water fountain. Once Tao and Caesar were sitting across from each other, the energy in the entire place shifted. They were like two lions in the running for one tribe.

"We have much to discuss," Caesar started.

"Do we?"

"Let's not pretend like there isn't an entire war going on around us. It has just begun. We can put an end to it before anybody else gets hurt."

"And what makes you think I care about everybody else?"

"We had peace before all of this. It would benefit each family to go back to that."

"The Tolliver family killed my uncle."

"And you killed Marco," Caesar said, and a fire lit in his eyes.

"Don't forget that I raided one of his warehouses, stole his shipment of weapons, and dispersed them to my men." Tao smiled, and Caesar turned his lip up.

"What did he do to you?"

"He sided with the enemy. Just like you."

"Do you really want to go to war with me, Tao? We both know what the end result would be."

"If you're implying that you would defeat me, then you are delusional. The Triad is on my side, and we are going to squash all of you. You were very smart for meeting me here. Are you afraid?"

"I could never be afraid of a pea when I am a giant," Caesar said, brushing Tao's threat to the side. "I only came to discuss the war. Not to see whose chest is bigger."

"And what is there to discuss, that there is no need for a war?"

"There isn't. I believe that we can all come to a resolve if we all get on the same page."

"You are not understanding me. There will be no peaceful resolve as long as you have anything to do with the Tolliver family. There's no way that my family will let the murderer of my uncle walk around still with breath inside of his body."

"Even if it means destroying the whole state?"

"We would rebuild. As long as we had full control."

"And see, that's where we differ. Do you know why I am content at having only Manhattan to rule?"

"I'm sure you are going to tell me."

"I am. When I was younger, all I saw was fighting between the families. Bodies pile up now, but back then it was ten times worse. I don't want to go back to that. Are you really foolish enough to think that if you truly can pull off killing us, there still won't be a war for the top spot? There won't be a night where you get a good night's sleep. By killing off all of your allies, you have nobody to watch your back. You'll always be looking over your shoulder. Do you really want to live like that?"

"Don't speak too quickly to say that I won't have allies. My grandfather is one of the most feared men in Hong Kong, and now I have his soldiers," Tao spat as he leaned forward. "None of you will be able to stand a chance against me. And you see them?" Tao pointed his finger toward Jin and Lan. "Those two can kill ten men without breaking a sweat or shooting a gun. Imagine what one hundred of them can do. You have no idea what you're in for."

"And neither do you," Caesar said with a smirk. "I don't know what kind of training these two gentlemen have had in their lifetime, but what I do notice is that neither one of them is your son. Where is he?"

Tao didn't say anything. There was something about the look in Caesar's eyes. It was a smug look, and not only that, but Caesar was smiling. It was not a happy smile, but a cunning one.

"If I had a son and he was missing for a few days, I know that I would not be sitting across from someone like me with the confidence that you have."

"How do you know he's been missing for a few days?"

"Because I've seen him."

"Where?"

"Here." Caesar pulled out his phone and opened something on the screen. "Green seems to be his color."

He slid the phone across the table for Tao to grab. When he did, he saw something that made him uneasy. And not because he saw a photo of his son bound to a chair and bleeding with green rope around his wrists. But because now Caesar truly did have the upper hand. If Chu On found out that Ming had been kidnapped under his watch, he could kiss everything he wanted goodbye.

"Release him immediately," Tao instructed.

"Now why would I do that when I seem to have you right where I want you? Since you don't want a peaceful resolve, how about a bloody one?" Caesar looked Tao directly in the eyes as he spoke. "You have two days to end this feud and present me and the other family heads with acceptable terms, or he dies."

He nodded his head at the men with him, and they knew it was time to go. Caesar left with Tao's dignity, leaving him with nothing but anger and his thoughts.

Chapter 31

Boogie knew how dangerous it was for him to be in the Bronx, especially at this time on a Friday night. But the information he needed was there, in Shen's condo to be exact, or at least he hoped it was. The high-rise building had a parking garage attached to it. Boogie was really careful as he pulled his car into it, making sure he didn't see any Asian faces. Even when he got out of the car, he put the hood of his black hoodie over his head and walked with his eyes on the ground. He had gotten Shen's address from Desire's appointment book, which he was happy about, because there was a chance that she hadn't even written it down since technically no one was even supposed to know about the meeting. That just showed how much Diana's teachings were embedded in her girls. He walked to the elevator and took it all the way up to the tenth floor. The hallway was well lit, and he walked down it, looking for door 1015. When finally he found it, he looked over his shoulder to make sure that nobody was coming or leaving. The coast was clear. From his pocket, he took out a few tools to unlock the door. It was the one thing in the world that he was extremely good at, and it only took him about fifteen seconds to open it.

The condo was dark, so he slowly eased inside. He listened to every sound to make sure that he was truly there alone. The only thing he could hear was the soft hum of the air conditioner. He shut the door behind him and turned on a light. The condo had a beautiful view, but that wasn't what he was there for. He closed the blinds and drapes so that if anybody was looking up, it would still seem like the lights were off. It smelled like cleaning products, as if somebody had come in there and scrubbed everything down. Boogie looked around and tried to decide where he wanted to start first. It was a nice place with champagne-colored furniture, marble floors, and a low-hanging chandelier in the dining room. The first places Boogie decided to check were the kitchen drawers. He didn't know about anybody else, but he knew that in black families they all had a junk drawer, a place where they kept all of the nothing and all of the same things. Unfortunately, Shen did not have one of those. Every drawer in the kitchen had a place for something and everything was neat.

Next up was the bedroom. The closer he got, the stronger the cleaning product smell got. He guessed that he had been killed in his bedroom.

"Hmm," Boogie said to himself when he was inside.

Shen's bed had been made, and everything inside was just like the kitchen—neat. Nothing seemed out of place, but something had to be. He got to work looking in every drawer in the dresser. And when he didn't find anything there, he moved to the bed, checking underneath it and the pillows. Once again there was nothing. There was a laptop sitting on the nightstand next to the bed. Curious, he opened it and powered it on. Maybe there was something there, but he was disappointed yet again. The hard drive had been completely wiped. Sighing, he placed the laptop back where he got it from.

The next place he went was to Shen's large walk-in closet. When he opened it, the first thing he laid eyes on was the assortment of suits. The different designers and fabrics caught Boogie's attention.

"This was a fly-ass motherfucka," Boogie said, touching an emerald green three-piece Balenciaga.

He thought his suit collection was hitting on something, but apparently not. Before he could get lost in admiring the clothes, he had to remind himself why he was there. He had to find something, but that was the hard part. He didn't know what he was looking for. He hoped that whatever it was would just jump out at him. But then again if it was that easy to find, he was sure Tao already had it. He searched the closet and tried to be careful not to take anything out of its place. He checked pockets, shoeboxes, even in between the oriental blankets he found on the top racks. Still he came up with nothing.

He found himself growing frustrated, and when he left the closet, he plopped down on the bed and kicked the mahogany nightstand next to it. Suddenly the side of the nightstand popped open, revealing a secret compartment. Almost not believing his eyes, Boogie was skeptical to look inside of it. But eventually he did, and he found a small firearm, a knife with engravings, and a disk. What caught him off guard was that the disk had his name on it.

"This has to be it."

Boogie removed the disk, popped it into the laptop, then pressed play. The video started, and he saw that it was some kind of security footage inside the dining room of a restaurant. Soon after, Tao came into the room and sat at one of the tables. He pulled out a piece of paper and his phone from the breast pocket of his suit. He looked from the piece of paper to the phone as he dialed a number, and Boogie turned the volume up so he could hear what was said. As he spoke, Tao changed his voice to where Boogie couldn't hear his Chinese accent.

"Hello, is this Boogie I am speaking to?" Pause. "It does not matter who I am. Just know I have some news for you. I understand that you want to see every head of the Five Families dead, besides yourself of course. I want to help you do that. Li will be lightly guarded when he arrives at his restaurant, Fortune, at around midnight. That is when you can take your shot. Don't miss."

He hung up the phone right after that. Boogie remembered the phone call. He hadn't even clocked that the person on the other end of the phone was Tao. Nor had he even thought to try to figure out who it was. Boogie watched as somebody else walked on camera. He almost fell off the bed when he saw who it was. Dina, his mother, sat next to Tao. She wore a big smile on her face and clapped her hands.

"Do you think he will do it?" Tao asked her.

"Of course he will. He's an idiot blind with rage. And when he's done, I trust that you'll keep up your end of the bargain."

"As soon as my uncle is out of the way and when I have controlling power in New York, you will have five million dollars in your account. That is, as long as you keep up your end of the deal as well."

"Trust me, when he does everything I need him to do, he'll be out of the picture. Boogie is a dead man walking."

"You could really kill your own son?"

"As easily as it was for you to put a hit out on your uncle."

The recording stopped after that, but Boogie's eyes stayed glued to the laptop screen. He wanted to say he didn't believe what he'd just seen, but he would be lying. After learning his mother's true colors, he wouldn't put anything past her, including conspiring with the Chinese.

"Damn," Boogie said to himself. "That's what Shen wanted me to know."

He was sure before, but he was positive now—Tao killed Shen to cover his own tracks. He was climbing his way to the top and leaving a bloody trail behind him. Boogie popped the disc out and made a phone call to Caesar. It rang all the way through to voicemail. He hung up and called another number.

"Talk to me," Nicky said when he answered.

"Yo, where's Caesar?"

"I think he's at the Big House, why?"

"I need to show him somethin'. I'm on my way there."

Chapter 32

"Who else knows about this?"

Caesar's voice was quiet when he spoke. He sat in disbelief watching and rewatching the video Boogie had brought to him. He could not believe how much he did not know Dina. No matter how he tried to understand, he just couldn't. Dina turned on her family in the worst way. She really would have traded Boogie's life for the thing she already had: money. Maybe she just wanted it without Barry and Boogie.

"I don't know," Boogie answered his question. "But I doubt Shen told anybody else. I think somethin' this big would have spread like wildfire."

"I think so too. This is big. Really big."

"You know what this means, right?"

"That Tao orchestrated this whole thing just so he could start a war."

"And once again my mother used me as the face of it."

Caesar could tell that he was trying to mask that sadness from his voice. The two of them were seated in the study of the Big House. Caesar had been trying to get his speech ready for the block party the next day when Boogie arrived. It wasn't hard to determine which one was more important. The speech would have to wait. Caesar went to where Boogie was sitting in a chair and placed a hand on his shoulder, squeezing comfortingly.

"I don't have any kind words to say about your mother. For the life of me I can't understand why she did the things that she did. I'm sorry."

"Ain't nothin' for you to be sorry about. She moved how she moved, and now we're here."

"There are plenty of things for me to be sorry about. And that is one of them. You shouldn't have had to go through anything like that. And now both of your parents are gone. I can't imagine how you might be feeling right now."

"I don't feel anything."

"Boogie—"

"Look, I'm not trying to be disrespectful, but that's not what I want to talk about right now."

"That was the problem you had before, isn't it? You didn't want to talk about your feelings. Instead you let the rage do the talking for you. I don't want that to happen this time. Tell me what you feel. I'm right here. Just talk to me."

"What the fuck am I supposed to say? How sad I am that my own mama got my dad killed and tried to take me out too?"

"Yes."

"And that even though I already knew who she was, it still hurt like hell actually hearin' her plot on me in that video?"

"Yes."

Boogie let his thoughts consume him until they turned into pure emotions. He felt anger, a lot of anger. But above all, he felt a sorrow so deep that nothing could fill it. His father was dead, and his mother couldn't have ever loved him. Roz and Amber were gone. He felt like he had nothing and nobody.

"I hate that she was my mama. I feel like everything was fake growin' up. When she looked at me, when she fed me, I keep wonderin' how many times she thought about killin' me. I just feel . . . I feel like I'm alone because I guess I am. These are the cards I was dealt though, so

I'm not gon' complain. I just have to live my life and keep going."

"You're right about living your life and keeping it going. But you're wrong about being alone. As long as I have breath in my body, you will never be alone. And now you have Morgan. And Nicky. And Lorenzo. But you have to feel that it's okay to lean on them."

Caesar stepped away from him and lit a cigar. He went back to the table he had been writing his speech on and moved the cards around with his hand. Suddenly a smile broke out on his face.

"What?" Boogie asked.

"Do you know the thing we lacked in our generation of running things?"

"What?"

"The all-around togetherness that you have with them. They naturally follow you, and Nicky hated you at first, but now you can't even tell. There's no power struggle even with all the shit that you did. They see you for you, not what somebody tried to make you out to be. They see your heart. Because even with all of the bad, you managed to bring us all together again. I'm learning that there never needed to be the Pact in the first place. All that we needed was for you to be born."

When Caesar spoke, all Boogie heard was his father's voice. He needed that. There was a lump that formed in the back of Boogie's throat. He swallowed it.

"Do you think I'll be okay?"

"I think you'll be just fine, son. You'll be just fine." Caesar took a big draw from the cigar. "But I think you'll be better if you can make up with your lady."

Boogie crinkled his forehead so fast in Caesar's direction, and Caesar burst out laughing. Boogie almost asked how he knew, because the only person he'd told was—

"Diana."

"She told me you were having trouble in the love department. She said she might not have been as helpful as she could have been. So let me offer you some more words of advice. Just because a woman isn't built for this life doesn't mean she is incapable of loving you through it. Sometimes it wouldn't hurt to see things from her point of view. It also wouldn't hurt going home early some nights."

"I can't."

"Try. The streets aren't going anywhere, but a good woman will leave your ass. So if she's worth it and you love her, try. Eventually your two lives will merge, and everything will be everything. Especially now that we have proof to show the leader of the Triad."

"You want to show him the video? Maybe he was in on it."

"As easy as I've been trying to take it in my healing state, it's been hard for me to sit back and do nothing. As far as Tao goes, I may not have hit him hard with force, but I've been doing my research and watching some of his moves. The leader of the Triad is here as we speak. He has lent Tao his army."

"Who is he?"

"His name is Chu On Yee, and he is Li's grandfather, which makes him Tao's great-grandfather. He is the leader of the Triad, and in his prime, he was one of the coldest motherfuckas to walk the face of the earth. He was trained in the ninja arts, and so is everyone under him. From what I have learned, Chu On is an honorable man, and I truly don't believe he would ever have his grandson murdered. Li was set to take over for him when he died as the leader of the Triad. The only person who benefits from his death is Tao because he gets to take Li's place. I gave him until today to come up with a peaceful resolve in order to save his son's life, but do you think he contacted me? No."

"So he's just gon' let his son die?"

"I don't think he cares if Ming lives or dies."

"I see why he and my mother were workin' together. They were the same person."

"I don't know when, but soon he's going to attack us with Chu On's army. And if that happens, the streets are going to be so hot it's going to feel like fire up our assholes. I can already see the destroyed businesses, the Feds on our asses, senseless death, and just complete chaos. It has to be stopped before it starts."

"So what are we gon' do?"

"Get word to Chu On about what Tao has been up to."

"But how?"

"I think I have an idea."

Chapter 33

Meditating didn't seem to be doing him any good anymore. Ming didn't know what day it was, how much time had passed, or if he would ever get out of there alive. His head hung weakly with his chin on his chest, and his breathing was rigid. His entire body ached, and bruises had started to form on his wrists from the green rope. The cracks on his dry lips burned, and he was parched. The foul odor of urine was constantly present in his nostrils. He hadn't been able to go to the bathroom, so he had to just go on himself. He reeked.

Caesar didn't make good on his promise to cut off his toes, but Ming did receive several beatings from his goons. He wanted information, but Ming didn't talk. He only told him what could be considered public knowledge about Chu On. One of his eyes was almost swollen shut, and he could feel a sting from a bloody gash on his right cheek. He knew Caesar was just keeping him alive to bait his father, but Tao was one of the toughest men alive. It would take more than threatening him with Ming's life to get him to bend to any will. Especially since Ming was trained to withstand and get out of situations like that.

The one thing that kept him going was the thought of killing the Kings and the Tollivers. He envisioned stabbing a knife through Boogie's chest and slitting Caesar's wrists. The same thing would follow for everyone they held dear. He could not wait to make them pay for what happened to his uncles. He flexed his wrist to see if the ropes around them had gotten any looser. And they had. He could turn his arms all the way around. All he needed was something sharp to cut himself loose. He looked around the room to see if he could find anything to hobble toward. Maybe some scissors or a knife. His eyes fell on a desk that wasn't too far from him. He started to gather his strength to work his way over there, but then he heard the sound of the library door opening. Caesar stepped inside and looked curiously at him. Ming returned the look by glaring at him with his good eye.

"Good, you're awake. The last time I came in here you were still unconscious from one of my boys knocking you out."

"My pain pleases you?" Ming asked in a weak and shaky voice.

"Hurting people never pleases me. Only a sick person gets joy from that. I only do what I have to do. And let's be clear—you asked for this. Your family has become a menace to society."

"And what do you consider yourself?"

"Not evil."

"Whatever," Ming spat. "If I'm still here, that means you need me for something. If I am not dead, it could only mean I am here to serve the purpose."

"You're too smart for your own good," Caesar said, puffing his cigar. "If you must know, I was using you as a bargaining chip. But that father of yours is a tough bastard. He was supposed to call me today with his terms for a peaceful surrender in exchange for your life. I never heard from him."

"That is because my father is filled with honor for his people. There is no way that he would let the man responsible for my uncles' deaths live freely. Even if that means sacrificing me."

"I thought the Chinese would do anything to get their own back. I didn't think sacrificing you would be an option."

"If my father feels that my getting captured was due to my own incompetence, he will leave it up to me to live or die. His focus is on the war. You all will rot, and he now has the manpower to make you do just that."

"Tell me something, Ming. Exactly *how* big are your people on honor?" Caesar asked, pacing back and forth in front of him.

"Is that even a question? Our honor is like a sheet of protective metal. We wear it proudly."

"Do you think that love and honor go hand in hand? I know your father doesn't."

"You don't know anything about my father."

"I've learned enough about him to know that he has no honor. And I've also learned enough to know that he doesn't love anybody."

"And you do?"

"I know that anything I do I own it. I don't try to cover my tracks by blaming other people. Anybody I love, I show them. I would never hurt them. Surely never kill them."

"I do not care about the words spewing from your mouth, Caesar King. When I am free of these binds, I am going to present you with the most painful death possible."

"I would laugh, but I'm curious. Why is it that you want to kill me so bad?"

"Your people killed my uncles. I want to hear you admit it."

"The most pitiful thing is it looks like you're the only person who genuinely cares about your uncles. And I wonder why. Listen, kid, you can want to kill me with everything in you, but there are some secrets that you need to know. The first is that we did not kill your uncle Shen. Neither Boogie nor my camp is responsible for making that call. Shen made a decision he thought was right and ended up dead because of it. The second is there is more to Li's death than we ever could have guessed."

"More? More like what?"

"What's done in the dark always comes to the light. Find out for yourself," Caesar said, and tossed two things into Ming's lap.

He looked down and saw a circular disc. He didn't know what that was for, but Ming felt his heart race at the sight of his uncle Shen's knife. How had Caesar gotten it? When he looked back up to ask, he found that he was once again in the library alone. That wasn't all.

Caesar had left the door open.

Chapter 34

The day of the block party in lower Manhattan had finally come, and as he said he would do, Nathan rode with Caesar to the event as his security detail. The main event took place in front of a building called Druid Hall, which was normally used to host meetings between government officials in New York. It was an honor to be hosted there. It was a little chilly outside, but that didn't stop the people from showing up. The line to get in was long, and Caesar couldn't tell a lie by saying it didn't feel good to see them all there to see him. There was food, face painting, and even people selling merchandise with his face on it. He had to admit the streets of Manhattan had always shown him love, even when at times he didn't feel he deserved it. It had been so long since he'd been in the field that he almost forgot. At first he thought it would be more than just a little risky to be out in the open like that, but security was heavily enforced. It would be like trying to break into Fort Knox to get to him.

"Ain't no Chinese motherfucka gettin' in here," Nathan commented as he stared out the window of the Rolls-Royce. "I doubt they would try anything knowin' you have one of theirs locked up though."

"I let him go," Caesar said, looking into his phone.

"You did what, Unc?" Nathan quickly turned his head toward him to see if he had heard right.

"I let him go."

"What would you do something like that for? Do you know I'm the one who caught him slipping? He could be after me."

"He could be after all of us. But for right now, I think he has his hands tied up with other things," Caesar said and just kept it at that.

The driver let him and Nathan out in front of the Druid building. It was a four-story building made of ashy white brick. There were about fifteen stairs that led up to the entrance of the building, and at the top of them were a podium and microphone. Behind them was a retractable banner with a photo of him on it.

"That's a good picture of me," he said before he got out of the vehicle.

The moment Caesar's feet touched the ground he was swarmed with security, and Nathan covered his six. They all bounded up the stairs and got Caesar inside of the building safely. There were refreshments inside and a few people standing off to the side having conversations. Boogie, Nicky, Lorenzo, Morgan, and Diana were already inside waiting for him. They were all dressed nicely, but Caesar instantly noticed Boogie's suit.

"Very dapper young man," Caesar commented in approval. "That emerald green looks good on you."

"I thought so too when I snagged it." Boogie grinned.

"The rest of you look great too. Thank you for coming out," Caesar said, acknowledging the rest of them, but then he turned to Lorenzo. "How are you holding up?"

"As best as can be expected," Lorenzo told him, but Caesar suspected there was more to it than that.

"We'll talk later," he said before Diana tugged on his arm.

"You're talking about them like you don't look good yourself, for an old man anyways," she told him with a wink.

"This old thing? It's just something I pulled out of the closet." Caesar ran his hand down the jacket of his brand-new Balmain suit. "I do clean up pretty nicely though, don't I?"

"You done got Unc started, Diana," Nicky joked.

"I guess I shouldn't make his head bigger than it already is," she teased and then looked at him warmly. "I don't know if I've ever said it, but I am so proud of you. From the moment I first met you, you have shown what a good man you were. I, like so many others, wouldn't be here if it weren't for Caesar King. You deserve every moment of shine you're about to get today."

"Thank you, Diana. I—"

"The man of the hour!" a booming voice interrupted him.

Caesar turned around and saw Mayor Jetson walking over toward them. He too was wearing a suit and a bright smile to match. The two men shook hands, and the mayor patted him on the arm.

"It's good to see you, man. I thought somebody had finally taken your old ass out."

"Now, Anthony, you've known me our whole lives. You should know it's going to take a lot more than some bullets to kill me."

"You're right, I should've known your ass was going to pop up somewhere. But I'll tell you what, I'm glad you did. Now I was just talking to your daughter, and she said you wrote quite a fine speech."

"Yeah, it's a nice one." Caesar said it with a straight face.

The truth was that Milli ended up writing Caesar's speech. He just couldn't come up with anything that was noteworthy, so she did it for him.

"Daddy!" Milli's voice came from nowhere. She ran up to her father and gave him a hug.

"Baby girl! When did you get here?"

"Not too long ago. When are you going to read your speech?" she asked and then saw the mayor standing there. Her voice suddenly got louder. "You know, the one that you wrote all by yourself."

Nicky and Boogie found themselves grinning. They knew what was up, and Caesar shot them a look that silenced them. But still they snickered under their breath.

"Oh, and, Boogie? Roz is outside looking for you," Milli told him.

"She is?" Boogie asked eagerly.

"Yeah. She's by the stairs."

"Bet," he said and left them.

"Caesar, I'm going to go outside and start prepping them for you. You know I'm up for reelection, so make me look good out there," the mayor said before walking away.

"And while he's doing that, I am about to go get some refreshments. That cake looks so good over there," Nikki said and made his way to the sweets table.

"I'm with him," Morgan said and followed him with Lorenzo in tow.

Nathan stayed put, surveying the scene like a hawk. When the mayor walked out the door, most of the people inside followed him out. Others lingered behind so they could finish snacking, but eventually they left too. Mayor Jetson's loud voice was muffled by the walls of the building as he gave his speech. However, they could all hear the cheering from the crowd outside. Diana moved and stood next to Caesar. She affectionately bumped her arm against his.

"It's not every day that a drug dealer gets this kind of recognition. You must feel like a real star."

"Don't worry, old lady. Your time to shine is coming soon."

"No, thank you. I've been shot once, and I don't ever want to do that again," she said, touching her rib cage. "Like you said, I'm an old woman. I may not look it, but I feel it. It's taking this wound so long to heal completely."

"Who are you telling? Just standing here hurts for me. I'm thinking about—"

"Retirement?"

"Are you reading my mind?" he teased. "But on a serious note, yes, I am. Not until I can leave Nicky with a fresh slate though. When he takes over, I don't want any of my shit lingering in the mist."

"That's exactly how I feel. I still am in shock about the revelation about Tao. He was behind Li's death the whole time?"

"It looks that way." After Caesar let Ming go, Caesar had called Diana and told her everything about Tao and about Dina.

"I wish Dina were still alive so I could kick her ass. She was a different kind of evil."

"She was. She left a lot of scars on her son that he'll have to heal himself. But I think he can do it."

"And what about the Chinese boy?"

"I did what I felt was right at the time," he said, and Diana nodded.

"Well, let's just hope that he isn't as stupid as his father."

At that moment, the mayor's assistant popped her head in and waved for Caesar to come out.

"Showtime," Caesar called and motioned for everyone to follow him. "Come on, everybody. I want you all to be out here with me."

Boogie had never had the jitters before when it came to approaching a woman, but for some reason, Roz had him so nervous. He'd called her the night before after leaving the Big House, and she didn't answer. There was so much he had to say, but he couldn't do it over her voicemail. Instead, he just told her where he would be the next day and when. He hoped she would show up, but he didn't know if she would. But there she was standing in front of a crowd at the bottom of the stairs, wearing a long-sleeved cream dress with her hair braided back. He could tell that she had taken her time on her makeup, and she looked stunning. A slow smile crept to her face when she saw him.

"Sup," she said when he was in earshot.

"I didn't think you were going to come. I know I called a little late last night."

"I'm glad you left a voicemail."

There was noise all around them, but they stood in silence for a while. Boogie didn't know what he wanted to say first. The last time he saw her she was walking out on him. Out of nowhere they both opened their mouths and started talking at the same time.

"Boogie—"

"Roz—"

"I'm sorry." She motioned her hands to him. "You go."

"Okay." Boogie grabbed her hands and looked into her beautiful eyes. "I guess I should start by sayin' I'm sorry. I realize now that all you needed was to be reassured. I know that you know I love you, but I never thought to put myself in your shoes with this shit. Bein' with a nigga like me gotta be the scariest shit ever. And maybe I'm selfish for askin' you to do it. If that's the case, I guess I'll be selfish then. Because I don't want to live without you."

"Oh, Boogie," she said dreamily and gently touched his cheek. "I love you so much. More than I ever thought I would. I shouldn't have left. I was just so flooded with emotions, you know? You're right. I don't know if I ever really thought about how much you come with, but having you makes it worth it. You love my child like she's your own, and she loves you back. I don't ever wanna lose that. I never wanna lose you."

She opened her mouth to speak some more, but Boogie silenced her by pressing his lips against hers. He kissed her for the world to see and didn't come up for air until he felt like it. After sharing their deep and passionate tongue dance, they embraced each other tightly. Boogie had missed the feel of her body against his. When they finally let each other go, Caesar was behind the podium preparing to make a speech. Boogie took her by the hand and led her to the top of the stairs to stand behind Diana and next to Morgan. Morgan's face lit up when she laid eyes on the two of them.

"So you're this Roz I've heard so much about," Morgan said and gave her a quick hug.

"Good things, I hope," Roz said and grinned up at Boogie.

"Great things," Morgan assured her. "We'll catch up after the speech. I'm so happy I have a sister and a niece!"

Her smile was so genuine that Roz gave her another fast hug before paying attention to Caesar. It felt good to see them interact and take to each other so well. Boogie felt bad for not bringing them together sooner. From the top of the stairs, he could see everything that was going on around him. Kids were running around playing, people were dancing to the music, but most returned and tuned in to Caesar.

"Good evening, everybody. I want to thank you all for coming out tonight," he started and looked down at the notes in his hands. "As most of you may know, I came back from the brink of death recently. Some of you didn't accept that I was gone, while others didn't believe it at all. I'm grateful to be able to come back to a community that cares so much. I have worked pretty much my whole life to build Manhattan into the great place that it is today. And I'm just so glad that I have more years to be able to do that."

Boogie heard all of his words. However, he was zoned out and watching the crowd. There was a specific movement that caught his eye. The majority of the people in the crowd were staying still and listening to the speech, but his eyes zeroed in on the black men in trench coats walking toward the stage. There were about five of them, and they were spaced out. It wasn't until Boogie got a clear look at one of their faces that he knew for sure something was wrong.

"Ain't that the nigga we had tied up at Marco's warehouse?" Nathan asked, noticing the same thing Boogie was. "Simon somethin'."

"Caesar!" Boogie shouted and tried to go for Caesar, but it was too late.

Shots rang out loudly before Caesar was even done speaking. Caesar ducked out of the way just as the podium was lit up with bullets. Screams filled the air, but still the gunshots were louder. The crowd dispersed frantically. The men Boogie had spotted had thrown their coats off and were shooting their weapons at them. Simon seemed to be aiming directly for him. Nathan got Caesar out of the way, and Boogie dived for Roz. They all fell back inside of the building.

"How the fuck did they get by security?" Nicky shouted.

"Because they're black like us," Nathan panted with his gun out. "You good, Unc?"

"I'm fine." Caesar rubbed his chin. "It makes sense now. Ming told me that when Tao killed me, he was going to kill everyone I love at the same time. He was talking about here at the block party. We were sitting ducks."

"And it wasn't hard for him to find out the location. The flyers were put up all over New York."

"We need to get out of here, Caesar," Diana said.

"I agree," Boogie said and turned to Roz, who was leaning against a pillar. "Come on, baby. We need to . . . Roz!"

She fell into his arms, unable to keep her balance. It wasn't until he caught her that he saw the torso of her dress was turning red from blood. She'd been shot.

"No no no no no. Baby. Baby, stay with me," he said, looking into her fluttering eyes. He fell to the ground with her, applying pressure to her wound with his hand. "Roz. Please don't leave me."

"Make sure Amber knows I love her," she said weakly.

"Tell her yourself. I'm not gon' let you die on me."

"Damn!" A voice echoed off the high ceilings. "That bullet was meant for you, but seeing you so hurt behind this bitch does my heart some good."

Simon Hafford was walking toward them. He must have come in through the back, and he wasn't alone. He had half a dozen black men with him who all had their guns pointed toward them.

"You better hope she doesn't die," Boogie warned.

"You should be happy you'll have a companion in the afterlife. Aht!" Simon suddenly focused his attention on Nathan, who had tried to aim his gun. Simon put the beam from his own weapon on Nathan's forehead and dared him to move. "I wouldn't do that if I were you. Drop it!"

"Bitch," Nathan said and let the weapon fall to the ground.

"Good boy. I'd hate to decorate Caesar's nice suit with brains. Not before you see the real man of the hour. Ladies and gentlemen! I'd like to introduce you to the true king of New York!"

There were more footsteps behind him, and appearing from around the corner was none other than Tao Zhang. He was wearing a baby blue two-button suit and a pair of sunglasses over his eyes. He wasn't alone. Behind him were at least fifteen Chinese men dressed in black. Boogie could tell by their stance that they were prepared to fight to the end. Tao looked from Caesar to Boogie as a slow and malicious smile crossed his face.

"Now the real celebration can begin."

Chapter 35

"Do you know how long I've waited and wanted to get all of you in one place?" Tao said and looked at them all almost hungrily. "Now that I have you, I almost can't contain myself."

As he spoke, Roz was laboring for breath on the floor next to Boogie. Morgan didn't seem to care that guns were pointed at them. She ran to her brother's side. She took over for him and applied pressure to Roz's wound.

"I got it," she said to him.

He didn't want to let her go, but there were snakes in the room that needed beheading. He kissed her on the forehead and said a silent prayer before standing back up. Blood was on his hands, and some had gotten on his suit, but he didn't care. Tao's eyes went to Boogie's attire, and recognition flashed in his eyes.

"Where did you get that suit?" he demanded.

"An old friend lent it to me. He's dead now though, but you knew that already," Boogie told him and stepped up to talk directly to Tao.

"What can I say? I don't do well with traitors around me."

Behind him, Nicky, Nathan, and Zo guarded Caesar and Diana. Nobody had made a move for their own guns, and Boogie could only assume it was out of fear of being shot before they had a chance to draw them. He was trying to think of a way he could get everybody out of the situation, especially Roz. She was bleeding out and needed medical help immediately.

"I wonder what your great-grandfather will do after he finds out about the traitorous thing *you* did," he said, trying to stall for time.

"I have no idea what you're talking about." Tao shrugged.

"Cut the shit. I know it was you who called me that night. That's the information Shen wanted to tell me. He caught you on camera plotting with my own mother."

The smile on Tao's face faded. His stare was so icy that Boogie swore he felt the frigidness. He had the look of a man who finally had a mirror held up to him. His secrets were out, and the only thing his track record proved was that he was out for only himself. He didn't care about his family. He showed that he would kill anybody and anything to get what he wanted.

"Are you taunting me?"

"No. Just stating facts. Do you want to know where your son is?"

"Already dead by now," Tao said and then looked at Caesar. "After you left me, I realized one thing. I will never jeopardize my entire operation for one man. Even if he's my son. I hope he had a quick death."

"You're just like my mother," Boogie said, getting his attention again.

"Ahhh, your mother. I never quite understood why she hated you so much. But she wanted you dead. Too bad she won't be around to see it happen."

"I'm not the one who's going to be dyin' today."

"Enough of this small talk," Simon spoke from beside Tao. "Let's just kill him already. All of them. You have a new empire to build."

"You're right. Kill them!" Tao motioned to both his and Simon's shooters.

"Didn't he just say he's not dyin' today?" a voice behind Tao and Simon shouted.

They turned around and were met by Bentley, Tazz, and Jerrod pointing automatic weapons at them. Boogie couldn't remember a time he was happier to see his right-hand man or his cousin. He didn't miss a beat. While his enemies were distracted, he pulled out his Glock and aimed it at Simon. However, he turned back around just in time and dived out of the way when Boogie pulled the trigger.

Boom!

The bullet missed Simon and struck one of his goons in the throat. Blood sprayed everywhere like a gruesome scene in a horror movie. Bentley, Tazz, and Jerrod let their rounds sing after that. They killed half of Tao's men instantly. Beside Boogie gunfire erupted as Caesar and Diana discharged their weapons as well. They were aiming at Tao, who had jumped out of the way and was shooting back at them.

"Unc!" Nathan shouted, seeing that Tao had a clear shot at Caesar's head.

He'd been busy fighting a Chinese man in hand-to-hand combat. But when he saw Tao about to shoot Caesar, he quickly put some lead in the man's head. He hurried to tackle Caesar out of the way just as the bullets flew by. They landed behind a large pillar, shielded from the gunfire. Boogie took cover behind one not too far from it with Diana.

"He's a slimy motherfucka," Diana said loudly over the gunfire as she reloaded her weapon.

She was breathing heavily, and Boogie saw her clutch her side. He looked back at the battlefield and saw Nicky holding it down with the others. The remainder of Tao's men had surrounded him like a shield. They were inching closer and closer to a side exit on the right, and the moment he was close enough, Tao took off running down the hall. Boogie made a move to go after him, but then he saw Simon running the opposite way.

"Cover me!" he shouted before leaving the security of the pillar.

A few bullets flew his way, but they hit the ground and walls around him as he ran. There was a fire lit inside of him, and the only way to put it out was with Simon's blood. Simon had run down a long hallway on the left side. Boogie could hear his footsteps echoing, but then they stopped. On each side of the hallway were doors that led to rooms, and Boogie could bet Simon had hidden inside of one of them. Boogie stopped running and started walking carefully. He pointed his gun inside of every door he passed.

"Come out come out wherever you are," he taunted. "It's time for you to die just like Shane and Shamar."

Boogie aimed his gun quickly inside a room on his right but was met with nothing but an empty room with a conference table and a dry-erase board. Suddenly he heard movement behind him. He tried to turn around, but it was too late.

"You should have looked left," Simon hissed, rushing from the room Boogie had his back to.

He knocked the gun out of Boogie's hand and sent a bone-crushing punch toward his face. Boogie dodged the hit, and as Simon's fist was whizzing past his head, he delivered a punch to the side of his ribs. Simon grunted in pain, but he still was able to move back quickly to avoid Boogie's uppercut.

"It hurts, doesn't it? Seeing someone you care about die," Simon breathed, throwing a jab at Boogie's chest.

The blow made Boogie stumble back, and Simon followed through with three more hits to his face. Boogie could taste the blood coming from his nose, but he didn't let up.

"Be quiet!" he bellowed and tried to take a swing at Simon, but he missed.

"I saw you outside with your tongue down her throat. You love her, don't you? I'm so happy I could rip your heart from your chest!"

Boogie thought about Roz back there lying and bleeding out. He had failed her. She had been right. He couldn't protect her. Simon had shot her because he was aiming for him. He wasn't her protector. He was the reason she was dying. But he couldn't let her die. He had to go back to her. Boogie felt a sudden surge of strength that not even he could explain. Simon charged toward him, and Boogie stepped left and swung as hard as he could. The blow he delivered to Simon's face was so powerful that Boogie heard his jaw crack. Simon fell to the ground, but Boogie didn't stop there. He ran to where his opponent had fallen and began to beat his face into the ground. A pool of blood formed under Simon's head, and he was dead long before Boogie finally stopped swinging.

Breathing heavily, Boogie looked down at Simon's lifeless body. He felt nothing. He'd just taken a life with his bare hands, and he felt nothing at all.

"Boogie!" he heard Morgan shout, and he took off running toward her.

When he reached her, he noticed that the gunfire had stopped. Nicky and Nathan were tending to Caesar and making sure he was okay while Bentley and Tazz were standing by Morgan and Roz. When he approached Tazz, they embraced.

"Thanks, y'all. You saved us."

"No problem, cuz. We were in the crowd when they started shootin', and then we saw them sneakin' around back."

"Yo, Boog. She needs to go to the hospital right now," Bentley said from beside his sister. He kissed her forehead. "You tough like Grandma. You ain't gon' die right here today. Understand me? I can't lose you too."

"I called the ambulance. She's lost so much blood," Morgan said. "I don't . . . She's alive, but I don't know for how much longer."

Right then, EMTs rushed inside of the building and paused, looking at the bloody massacre. They didn't know where to start. Everyone was dead except one.

"Over here!" Morgan shouted. "Please help her."

"Please," Boogie said.

They rolled a stretcher over to her and carefully put her on it. Her eyes were fluttering at that point, and she was so weak that her arms just fell from her stomach. It was the worst pain in the world for Boogie to see her like that. Two men rolled her away quickly.

"Any close family members want to ride in the ambulance?" a female EMT asked.

Boogie looked at Bentley, and he shook his head.

"I'ma just meet y'all at the hospital. I need to do some damage control. You go."

"You sure? She's your sister."

"Go! You're wasting time, nigga."

Boogie didn't need him to say it a third time. He ran with the EMT outside and started praying. He held Roz's soft hand in his and didn't let it go, even when they were in the back of the ambulance.

I promise I'll be a better man. Just please don't take her from me. Please!

Chapter 36

Tao had fled the scene of his failed attack and cursed himself as he walked through the door of his mansion. He would have to send somebody to recover the bodies of the fallen before it could come back that they weren't United States citizens. The house was dark, but he could still make out things as he maneuvered. He needed to go to his office and have a drink.

He was more than angry. He was embarrassed. How had such a foolproof plan gone wrong? It was his fault for underestimating his enemy, but still he could not bring himself to place the blame on himself. It was that idiot Simon's fault. How had he not watched the door and seen those three walk in? Even with the best training in the world, Tao's men were no match for AK-47 assault rifles. He could taste the scotch on his tongue as he grew closer to his office door. He was glad Chu On's bedroom was on the other side of the house. He would inform him of what had happened in the morning, after he came up with a clever way to tell him that the blacks had ambushed them.

When he got to his office door, it was shut, which was not out of the norm. However, he saw a dim light coming from under the door. That was odd because he was positive that he turned every light off before he left the last time. He entered the room and was shocked to see Chu On standing next to his desk. Tao looked around and didn't see anybody else.

"Great-grandfather, is everything okay?"

"I should be asking you that. I saw on the television what happened today. My men were killed."

"You gave them to me, so technically they were my men."

"They were killed nonetheless. You were not smart. How do you explain this?"

"We were ambushed," Tao said quickly, going to pour himself a cup of scotch.

"How can you be ambushed at an event that was not yours? You were the one doing the ambushing."

Tao didn't say anything. He just tossed the liquid back. He welcomed the hot sensation down his throat. The old man stood there giving him a disgusted look, like Tao was the lowest of scum. Chu On spat at the ground.

"What?" Tao asked and placed the glass back down on its shelf.

"When I am gone, I want somebody who is fit to lead to take my place."

"It is just one battle, great-grandfather. To think the war is lost is foolish."

"Since I have been here there has not been one piece of good news brought to me. First I hear that my other grandson, your son, is kidnapped."

"Who told you that?"

"You forget that the men who surround you now are only borrowed. Their loyalty will always lie with me until I die."

Tao thought back to his meeting with Caesar. Jin and Lan had been in earshot the entire conversation. There was no doubt in his mind that, when they returned, they reported what they had learned to Chu On.

"What does not sit well with me is that you did not try everything in your power to get him back," Chu On continued.

"There is no point trying to save a finger when I am focused on the whole hand."

"What about if that finger is a thumb? The most crucial finger. You are foolish like your father. All of the training you gave your son you should have been giving yourself. You lack discipline. All of your greatest desires are selfish. A good leader focuses on his family, but you? You only focus on yourself. I never liked you."

"You don't have to tell me what I already know. You never liked my father either. I'm sure that's why you did not care for me."

"No, I did not care for you because I saw your inside at an early age. It is not because of your father. I enjoyed your brother. He was not a leader, but he had a good heart. Where is he?"

The way he asked the question made it sound rhetorical. He just watched every part of Tao's face in search of a reaction. There was something about the look in Chu On's eyes that told Tao that he knew something, but how could he? He couldn't have. Nobody knew what he had done to Shen.

"Great-grandfather, maybe we should finish this discussion in the morning. I am very tired, and I must think of my next course of action. What happened today was unacceptable, and next time I have to hit harder."

"You do not dismiss me. I dismiss you. I think we should discuss it now."

Tao felt himself go impatient. He was tired of respecting a man for nothing. The only reason he put up with Chu On was because he wanted to take his place. But there they were alone. If something were to happen to him inside of his great-grandson's home, nobody would suspect foul play. He was so old that it was only a matter of time before he croaked anyway.

"Where are your guards, Great-grandfather?" Tao asked, moving closely to him.

"They are around."

"Nowhere close though, right?" As Tao passed a couch along his office wall, he grabbed a decorative pillow.

He could suffocate the old man and carry him to his room. In the morning he would say he died in his sleep. He would send word back to Hong Kong and be crowned the new leader of the Triad by right. He didn't even feel the creepy smile that spread on his face.

"I don't understand the nature of these questions," Chu On asked right as Tao got close enough to grab him.

"It's because he wants to kill you, Great-great-grand-father."

The voice shocked Tao, and he stopped moving all together. He would recognize that voice anywhere. It was his son's. Ming spun around in Tao's desk chair and faced him. He looked like he had been to hell and back. Still, Tao could see the hateful look on Ming's beaten-up face.

"Son. You have returned. When?"

"I was released from Caesar's clutches last night. But I did not arrive home until this evening."

"Released?" Tao was confused.

"He let me go."

"He just . . . let you go?"

"Yes. When he saw that you were not going to budge peacefully in the war, he let me go."

"You must have told him something," Tao accused him. "Caesar King is not the type to just let a prisoner go. Not alive anyway."

"Well, he did. And on the contrary—he was the one who filled me in on some things."

"Things like what?"

"Like about who my father really is." Ming's eyes were on fire. "A murderer of his family. A man with no honor."

"You don't know what you speak of. Shut your mouth."

"I wish what I said were not true. You trained me to be an honorable warrior, yet you do things like this?"

Ming grabbed a small black remote from Tao's desk drawer and turned on the overhead projector in the office. He instantly recognized his Chinese restaurant and himself on the screen. He listened to his own voice tell Boogie where he could find Li to kill him. His body grew tense, and his jaw muscles tightened. He was caught.

"You ran here to show Chu On this?"

"He needed to know the truth. We all did. You killed Shen, too. Didn't you?" Ming asked.

Tao slowly turned back to him. As he stared at Ming, his own flesh and blood, he didn't see his son. He saw just another man.

"He was weak. Like you. He was going to betray me. So he got what was coming to him."

"You are a monster."

"Then what does that make you? In many ways you are just like me," Tao reminded him. His chest moved up and down as a crazy laugh escaped his lips. "I did not expect to have to kill the last of my remaining immediate family, but nothing will get in the way of my destiny. Great-grandfather, I'll lead them well. I will tell them that I came in here and it was too late. Ming had already killed you and so I had to kill him. What a sad story, don't you think?"

He dropped the pillow and reached for the gun on his waist. Before he could even aim it, there was a loud gunshot. Shortly after, he felt a burning sensation in his abdomen. He looked down and saw blood seeping out of his body. He touched the wound and brought his bloody fingers to eye level as if to make sure it was really blood. He looked back at Ming and saw him holding a smoking .22 that Tao kept in his desk.

"I am nothing like you. I will never trade my honor for money or power."

Tao began to feel lightheaded and dizzy. He stumbled back and fell onto the office couch. Chu On walked slowly over to him and snatched the gun from his waist. He spat at Tao's feet before resuming his position at Ming's side. He focused all of his attention on Ming.

"You, great-great-grandson, are fit to lead. This borough is yours. And when I die, you will rule Hong Kong. But first, you must prove yourself worthy."

"How, Great-great-grandfather?"

"This place, New York, is the perfect place to expand to. But we cannot rule over an oversaturated place. You must finish what your father started. You must take over every borough."

Ming hesitated at first. But after the shock settled, he nodded his head.

"I will. But first I have one more loose end to tie up," he said and pointed the gun in his hand at the center of Tao's forehead. "Goodbye, Father."

He squeezed the trigger one time, and the bullet struck its target, decorating the office in red.

The End

Book 4 coming soon . . .